SAN DIEGO PUBLIC LIBRARY
3 1336 00719 06
D0016807

The Romantic

Also by Aram Saroyan

Aram Saroyan
Cloth: An Electric Novel
Genesis Angels: The Saga of Lew Welch and the Beat Generation
Last Rites: The Death of William Saroyan
O My Generation and Other Poems
Pages
Poems
The Rest
The Street: An Autobiographical Novel
Trio: Portrait of an Intimate Friendship
William Saroyan
Words & Photographs

Aram Saroyan

The ROMANTIC

McGraw-Hill Book Company

New York St. Louis San Francisco Bogotá
Hamburg Madrid Mexico Milan Montreal
Panama Paris São Paulo Tokyo Toronto

Grateful acknowledgment is made for permission to quote the following copyrighted material:

Epigraph by Robert Graves from "Nothing Now Astonishes," published in *Collected Poems, 1975*, © 1975 by Robert Graves. Reprinted with the permission of Oxford University Press.

Lines from "I Want to Know What Love Is," written by Mick Jones. © 1984 Somerset Songs Publishing, Inc. Original recording: Foreigner. Used with the permission of E.S.P. Management, Inc.

1 2 3 4 5 6 7 8 9 FGR FGR 8 9 2 1 0 9 8

ISBN 0-07-054859-5

Library of Congress Cataloging-in-Publication Data

Saroyan, Aram.
The romantic: a novel / Aram Saroyan.
p. cm.
ISBN 0-07-054859-5
I. Title.
PS3569.A72R6 1988
813'.54—dc19 88-16916
CIP

Book design by Patrice Fodero

Rest, my loud heart. Your too exultant flight
Had raised the wing-beat to a roar
Drowning seraphic whispers.

—Robert Graves

The Romantic

1

He woke up in their new bedroom. Next door his older daughter's radio alarm clock had just gone off and he was suddenly awake and "going down, down, down, down" with Mr. Springsteen, until this passage was abruptly truncated. His daughter had turned off the radio and now was moving about her room, sliding her closet door open and closed, opening her bureau drawer, getting dressed for school. At fourteen her footfall was heavier than her mother's, perhaps heavier than his own. He lay in their bed, listening to the birds and from time to time gazing through the open window at the end of the room. White mist rose off the green expanse of the lawn in the early morning sunlight. It was October.

In a little while, Lisa went downstairs, and he got up from their bed, trying not to disturb Betty with too abrupt a movement. It would be fifteen minutes or so before his younger daughter, Stephanie, who was eleven, would be getting up to her own music. And his nine-year-old son, Paul, would be another half an hour still—unless, as sometimes occurred, he woke, and his feet thudded to the floor and he padded urgently to the toilet for his morning piss. But there was no noise and he decided to skip his robe. Naked, he walked through the hall to their big second-floor bathroom, the old sugar maple outside filling the window with its yellow. In a moment, he was in the shower.

Out of the shower, the bath towel now wrapped around his waist, he shaved, applied Pierre Cardin after-shave and deodorant and then, remembering his schedule, clipped the hairs from his nose and his ears. At forty, back from the outlands of the civilized world, a northern California enclave where the sixties still hadn't ended, James—who was a playwright who had become a screenwriter—needed consciously to pursue these niceties. After all, what if he forgot and exposed himself—if not to ridicule, exactly, to the more insidious, because entirely tacit, censure of the people with whom he did business? Or was that strictly paranoia? Look at Reva, for God's sake. As he was heading back to the bedroom, the phone rang. Assuming it was Mark, Paul's friend from down the street, he picked it up off the wall receiver just outside the open door to Paul's room. He could see his son sprawled diagonally across his bed, still asleep.

"Hello?"

"Listen, let's knock back a couple of tall, cool ones and dig Sonny Rollins." This was followed by deep laughter.

It was Henderson, another writer in their Connecticut town, also newly arrived. After years of cranking out a yearly detective novel, he had suddenly, apparently on the basis of his latest, *Shot,* which showed no appreciable difference in style, been lionized by *The New York Times Book Review,* and the book had been bought by Hollywood. His long fuse, extending over the two decades of his career, was now burning dangerously close to the explosive center of his normally wry, under-wraps persona. Like many big men, he was shyer than his size indicated, though shyness didn't seem to have much hold over him at the moment.

"It's barely seven thirty in the morning. What are you talking about?" Looking at the intricacies of a small Miró drawing on the wall opposite the telephone, James held the tuck of the towel around his waist as Stephanie passed him in her nightgown on her way to the bathroom.

"Hey, buddy, you're talking to the proud owner of a soundproofed basement rec room outfitted by the Audio Police. I gave the dude carte blanche. Anyway, dig it, Sonny in the garden at the Museum of Modern Art, 1965. 'There Will Never Be Another You,' Billy Higgins doing incredible things with the brushes and the high hat. You can hear every ricochet. I'm telling you, kid, it's bebop, and it's *back.*" Another deep laugh.

He decided to take this in a relaxed manner, see what shape things might take from here. "Sounds great, Rick," he answered in his mildest Mr. Lucky voice. "But I've got to see my agent for lunch, and before that I'm seeing this magazine editor. How 'bout a rain check?"

"Magazine editor? I thought you wrote movies."

"Yeah, this is just for fun." Now he turned and leaned against the doorframe of Paul's room, looking at the white birch tree in the garden. The mist had evaporated; it would be a beautiful day.

"Hittin' the city, huh? I'd almost go with you, but I did it yesterday. Scored some grass, Columbian sinsemilla; absolutely free of paraquat, take my word for it. Who's your agent—Swifty?"

Case closed: Rick was stoned. Was that why he could suddenly hear traces of a Southern accent he had never noticed in his speech before? "No, Reva Makepeace at Creative Clients."

"Makepeace, Makepeace...big girl?"

"Yeah. She's around my height."

"And knows karate?"

"Not that I know of. Rick, I gotta go..."

He laughed again; then added: "Just kidding."

James assumed this referred to the comment about Reva knowing karate, but maybe he meant the whole call. "Go easy on the killer weed," he said by way of wrapping up.

"Haven't smoked it in years, and you know what? This time around no paranoid reaction. None. How about that?"

"Great, I guess. Where's Mary?"

"Asleep. I only called because I knew one of you'd be up with the kids. Hey, this is nice, this morning trip around here."

"You ought to try it some time after a night's sleep."

"Okay, killer, enjoy your lunch."

He hung up and walked into the bedroom to dress.

Since he had to be up, he would let Betty sleep and get the kids off to school himself.

Downstairs, Lisa was sitting at the dining room table with *The New York Times*. In the kitchen, James put some water on for coffee, and began to fry some bacon on low for Stephanie and Paul's breakfasts. He filled a bowl with Cheerios, sliced a banana over it, added Light 'n Lively, and headed for the dining room table. He put the bowl down, got a place mat out of the Early American pine chest of drawers, and brought it to the table and set the bowl on it. He went back to the chest for a spoon and the honey jar, and then came back and sat down. There was a half-eaten piece of raisin toast left on Lisa's plate, and a little orange juice left in her glass. She was reading a review of a Sting concert.

"How was he?"

"Fine," she answered as if the question were slightly absurd and without looking up at him.

"Now..." he hesitated, seeking the right words, "I want you to do me a favor today."

"I know what you're going to say, and I don't want to talk about it."

"You *don't* know what I'm going to say." But he didn't want to sound angry. He looked up from his bowl, past the bouquet of pink tulips in the center of the table, at the sun-filtered room with the Dufy etching of heaven on the far wall. "Notice we're living in a sort of paradise?" Instantly, he heard the sanctimoniousness of his tone and knew these weren't the words he was seeking.

"I hate it." She still hadn't looked up from the paper. She was beginning her sophomore year at the high school; her first year there, beginning just after they'd moved to town and before they'd bought the house, had gone well academically, but not socially.

"That's because you're waiting for a police escort into friendship or something. They don't give those."

"Just shut up, okay?" She looked over at him now with clear-cut hatred.

"Look, I'm not asking you to break down doors. You said *she* asked *you* to have lunch…"

"But then she forgot." She had gone back to the *Times.*

"So what? So she didn't remember? You can ask *her* now. Or call her."

"Just stop it, will you? I told you—I don't know her last name."

Outside the dining room window, a red bird swooped low and then perched on a branch in the dogwood tree. Was it a cardinal? Lisa looked over at him and, he knew, was about to leave the table. "I just want to say one thing."

"No!"

His daughter was beautiful; she had her mother's features, his coloring, and then something all her own. Her face could darken and lighten like weather, and with the freshness of weather. "Tiny thing?"

"No!"

He thought he detected a hint of a smile. "Itsy-bitsy little—"

"No!" she shouted, turning around to face him

squarely, and then couldn't help smiling while at the same time standing up. "I've gotta go."

He'd get it in tonight. He wanted to tell her that she wouldn't feel bad even if she got refused by the girl, which he knew wouldn't happen. She wouldn't feel bad even if it did happen, though, because she'd have put herself out. Or *would* she feel bad? Maybe he was lucky she hadn't let him get it in, after all.

After she'd gone, he took the newspaper, put it in order, and scanned the front page. A possible war in Nicaragua? Americans didn't want a war so how could that be? American-trained and -sponsored contras committing atrocities and blaming them on the Sandinistas so the Reagan administration could justify armed intervention to Congress, as James had read in *The Nation?* Or maybe the Sandinistas really had done some of those things, as he had read somewhere else? Who could tell him?

He turned to the movie section to see the ad. It was going into major release throughout the tri-state area today and they had run a week-long campaign of larger and larger ads to gear up for it. Today's was a whole page, headlined by the quote from *People:* "*London Bridge* has the topsy-turvy joie de vivre of all screwed-up youth. It will make you feel good." He felt something on his left and turned to find Stephanie standing beside his chair, still in her blue flannel nightgown.

"Gosh, another ad," she said sleepily. "Gosh, that's great, Dad."

"Thanks, Stephie. Hey, aren't you supposed to be dressed?"

"Nooo," she said, stretching. "You *think* you know my schedule, but you don't." Now she stretched more luxuriously, and smiled at him. She was just a little taller than he was sitting in the chair. "I'm so glad it's Friday."

"Why?" He smiled.

"Oh, because tomorrow I can stay in my warm bed as late as I want; all cozy, see?" She giggled.

He could hear water boiling in the kitchen. He got up to make a cup of coffee as she went on to the basement to get clothes out of the drier. Stephanie was their little artist and resident sensualist. She and Paul regularly raged and beat on each other; and then, calm restored, usually by Betty or him, ventured into Monopoly games that could last for days, or delved into the still unfamiliar neighborhood on their bikes. Now, with Mark, Paul had found a steady friend in the neighborhood, and Stephanie was understandably ambivalent about this alliance. James turned over the bacon strips. Now he brought together cup, saucer, and spoon, added a level teaspoon of Taster's Choice Maragor Gold Blend, and poured the boiling water from the stove into the cup. Suddenly Paul was standing in the middle of the kitchen, his blond hair completely disheveled, and naked except for his underpants.

"The Yankees lost," he said with a weariness.

"Again?" James was adding milk and sugar to the coffee.

"Yeah. I heard it on the radio."

"I guess they can't catch up anymore now, can they?"

"Well, they *could,*" Paul answered, his fan's heart momentarily astir.

Holding his coffee cup, James began to move slowly back out to the dining room while his son, still ruminating, stood in a patch of the room's morning sun.

2

He parked the Mercedes in the Eighty-eighth Street garage between Park and Madison. Walking down Madison Avenue, the buildings looming grayly in his peripheral vision, he passed a wall of posters, including three in a row for *London Bridge,* his name, among others, glowing in the pale midmorning sunlight. There were posters like these all over the city just now, and he couldn't pass one without paying at least a beat or two of subliminal attention. There was a parallel of sorts, it had struck him, with whatever satisfaction a graffiti artist knew in having his mark spray-painted, like personal punctuation, throughout the corridors of the city. You were, in a certain sense, home.

A young mother wheeled her baby up from the Eighty-sixth Street corner as he walked downtown past the Madison Delicatessen (the scene of so many testy, taciturn dinners with his father during his last years). Smart, brunette, with an oversized dark blue turtleneck, the woman nevertheless had the slightly imperious, somewhat clinical look of young mothers: their parts, formerly purely for pleasure, now enlisted in Nature's Plan. Yet, unexpectedly, she looked up and smiled rather shyly at him as he walked by.

It was a cavalcade of—if not stars (and, after all, New York was where they all still *walked,* Warren, Jack, Diane, and Angelica), then of that substrata he himself preferred: the stylish anonymous of New York, the most stylish anonymous anywhere in the world, although right here on the Upper East Side wasn't quite the fun-city precinct of, say, the Upper West Side, or virtually any other Manhattan neighborhood. It was because here you had the real marathoners: the young who had taken it all in deadly earnest, no ifs, ands or buts, and come out on top, the most expensive neighborhood in the world. Then again, occasionally you passed an old woman of such blistering, undisguised and (therefore?) regal ugliness it might have frozen the mind. But you had to maintain that New York rhythm of awareness that didn't admit sustained attention, or at least not on a single object, while mobile. Rather, the meditation was in the movement, the switching from visage to visage, as you kept up the pace. There was a music to it, the mind and muscles picking up a certain beat and not suffering an alteration gladly. Just last week, about to walk with Betty and the kids across Seventy-ninth Street and Madison, he had spied a bum on the downtown side of the street with his penis out and, with a quick look to Betty, detoured everyone across Madison without putting an obvious crimp into their group rhythm.

In fact, wasn't there supposed to be less honest-to-God fucking going on in New York than in most places in the world—had he really read this in the Living section of the *Times?* Something about career pressures subsuming the juices. When he was writing a play he got into bed at night without a buzz on his body, all the lights on his peninsula subject to brownout in the storms of creation. Now, on the other hand, something was causing a lot of buzzing.

Maybe, he thought, passing a fantastic Picasso in the window of a gallery on the corner of Seventy-fifth Street—a one-eyed woman with a beckoning in all her various parts (now *he* was the painter of passion, the terrible Spaniard and a half)—maybe it was because, with all the compromises and reversals, the power failures and personal blackouts that had ensued in his transformation from an off-Broadway playwright into a mainstream screenwriter, he was somewhat uncertain of his own reality, in the end. He had done what he was told to do; past a certain point, he had stopped arguing. He wanted the money and they gave it to him and he stopped being a fountain of paradoxical intelligence, and settled for working his ass off for Annette Reed, the director, who knew how to get a movie made. A human spark plug, tiny, dark, and operating on an erotic frequency he had never deciphered (except perhaps that it was work and work alone), she had taken to calling him, looming over her and four years her senior, "kid."

The oddness of the feeling had a lot to do, no doubt, with its sexual indeterminacy. Only a few hours before one of his work sessions with Annette, he might have been fucking his brains out in the midnight sun with Betty. Then again, maybe not. One night Betty had been tired or out of sorts, and, the rest of the darkened household also oblivion-bound, he'd switched on the cable station to see Lisa de Leuwes passively-aggressively making a banquet of her prodigious endowments for the first available male. There he was in the dark, then, lying beside his sleeping wife watching this woman make herself wickedly apposite the perennial male fantasy. Was she on drugs or what?

Annette, on the other hand, was Miss Hollywood hardball, and he felt a gnawing, eunuchlike indefiniteness in her presence. She was a woman he wasn't ever going to fuck, that was usually crystal clear, and that status, albeit that he was a faithful married man, nevertheless comprised an instant subtraction from his usual range of being. Who cut the lights?

Walking up the hill at Seventy-second Street, he decided to take in the Fairfield Porter exhibit at Hirschl & Adler (he could let Betty know the extent of it before her next visit to the city). He still had almost an hour before he was due at the *Manhattan* magazine offices.

On the other hand, maybe the buzzing had to do with the fact that he'd now "taken care of business," and that comprised some kind of decompression. His family was in a house with central heating. The kids had good shoes. Betty had, for the first time in their life together, a studio of her own. He stepped from the street into the small, empty, tiled lobby. He walked the echoing length of it and pressed the elevator button and the door sprang open. He rode up one floor and walked a few steps and into the gallery.

* * *

Just after entering, he encountered a portrait Porter had painted of his retarded son. The boy, seen seated at the piano, looked to be about twelve, and something in the portrait made it clear that his interaction with the piano, and everything else, was in some way abbreviated, truncated. At the same time, as he had encountered in a mongoloid girl in their town in Marin, there was something luminous in the boy's spirit, something all-giving in a language that existed prior to the one learned. Somehow Porter had rendered the colors of the room, his son, and the piano in a way that gave each a kind of heightened separateness, an individual obdurateness. One could imagine the music of the mad suddenly erupting over the room's civilized harmonies. But the painter had also achieved an uncanny balance, the elements all in fundamental equipoise, like the life Porter had achieved that embraced his son.

James walked into the gallery at large, removing his scarf and tucking it into the pocket of his dark tweed jacket, thinking of Betty and their children with a sudden rush of love.

Walking down Madison again, with the traffic in his ears, he turned east, heading in a roundabout way toward the editorial offices of *Manhattan.* Reva said the editor there, Kate Warners, was trying to make the magazine more of a writers' showcase and had loved *London Bridge* and wanted to meet him and discuss a possible piece. The money, considering what they were asking for, was remarkable. Then there was Warners's voice on the phone: softly patrician, a Seven Sisters voice, and he was curious to see what she looked like.

Was it that he had been locked up too long with a town full of loud women who held weekly meetings to discuss their acid trips? At a certain point it had dawned on him that this California town's real power axis was ruled by single women in their middle years whose earlier adult life (usually as homemakers) had been broken by the 1960s. Now in their forties, they threw parties, dropped acid, sponsored consciousness-raising sessions, and took up with younger men. They were, through either the male or the female side of a marriage, a potential threat to it. They also kept the sixties going long past its actual duration in letter or spirit. As late as the mid-seventies, certain women of their town had even renamed themselves: Selma Estabrook, a former member of SDS from the Bronx, had converted to Silva Mind Control and was now known as Bluejay. Olive Rackstraw, from one of Westchester County's richest families, lived in a bus and was known as Undertow, an apparent reference to her persona on acid.

In any case, since his new script, *Success!*, was being batted around by the studio heads, he had the excuse that he might as well make a little pocket money, or at least see what Warners had in mind. Park Avenue, with its gleaming glass monuments reflecting blue sky and the buildings opposite, loomed before him. Oh yes, the name of the game was money. The article he might or might not choose to write would pay him close to a third of what he had made during an average year of their California sojourn.

3

Kate Warners turned out to be a dark-eyed brunette, quite tall, with a delicate bone structure. What was *he,* though, an ornithologist? Sighted: a black-wing literary bird. Location: fifth floor, Seventy-sixth Street and Second Avenue. Details: hesitant, with a nice smile. No, it was just that, after all those years chopping firewood, he had, in the presence of this oh-so-citified specimen of the female, the bracing notion that he was almost the uncouth woodsman, Mellors to this Lady Chatterly in a simple black dress.

They sat in her corner office, batting a few ideas back and forth—most prominently a profile on the actor who had come to public acclaim in *London Bridge,* a young man whose ruling ambition seemed to involve a succession of *Playboy* and *Penthouse* centerfolds, the page made flesh. Bobby Franco.

"Bobby's—a possibility," he said politely. "But I don't really know him."

"But that's the point, isn't it?" Warners answered with her Seven Sisters cool.

"How do you mean?" He sat up now and laced his fingers in front of him. Time for the yokel to get organized. Here we are, guy, all ten fingers at your command.

"Well, I mean I've run into him at the Palladium but—nobody does, do they?" Warners asked ambiguously.

"Know him, you mean?"

"Well, I mean other than biblically?"

Tut tut. "Yes, he's definitely a Bible study, Bobby."

"So I gather," Warners added with her smile, suddenly looking him up and down.

Betty loved his muscles—she remembered him from a time when he hadn't had them—but Betty was quite strong herself. Warners, on the other hand, he would have to be careful to embrace delicately. This was definitely male-chauvinist madness creeping over him now, King Kong and Fay Wray stuff. No doubt that was the secret of the movie's timeless appeal: man's ceaseless quest to dominate his other half.

"Hey, here's a thought."

"Good," Warners answered.

What must have been an enormous vehicle passed below on Second Avenue, causing clangs and tremblings in the atmosphere.

"You know what I do in New York?"

"What?"

"Promise not to tell?" Would she let him put on his charm hat? Let's get happy.

"Promise."

"I haunt specialty secondhand bookstores all over town, just about all of them. And maybe..."

"That might be a piece. We could get a good photographer..."

"Oh, you'd *want* photos. There's a little basement shop up on Eighty-fourth Street, the Brazen Head, and the guy's hand-picked every title. Very picturesque."

"Interesting." She looked serious.

"Well, look..." Suddenly he probably had been hired, which completely reversed the electrical current in the situation. He'd enjoyed ten or fifteen minutes during which Warners was trying to capture his fancy; now he'd put himself under her auspices. He wanted to walk back into the previous moment. "Why don't you let me think about it."

"Yes, think about it." She smiled a smile that introduced a sort of suspended animation. Maybe he was to do his thinking in the moment? Right here?

"Or maybe," he essayed, "*you* could think about it, or we could both think about it together..." Easy does it, now.

"I could do that." She inhaled here, always a wonderful event to him when a pretty woman made it visible. The world was his box of chocolates.

"You don't happen to ski, do you?" she asked, smiling.

"No, but I fuck." *Damn* it. What was *happening* to him?

Yet she seemed unalarmed. "Do you always talk like a teenager when you're alone with a woman?"

"A teenager? I'm sorry, what age would you prefer?" But he was grateful, after all, that she hadn't screamed for the police.

"How old *are* you?"

"About forty."

"About?"

"Well, it seems to be some kind of threshold I'm just inside of... I mean not *all the way* inside of..."

"I think that's all right," she answered benignly.

"I'm not sure I understand." The question was, with the abrupt internal commotion he had just set off in this day-bright, paper thin, eleven-in-the-morning office, punctuated by typewriters and telephone lines, whether they might be getting down to blood. His own, yes. His heart was now pounding with fear, although there was a paradoxical stirring in his groin, too. The phone on her desk buzzed and, after a moment with her secretary, she took a call from someone about something he could understand only obliquely, and when she hung up, she looked back at him and exhaled visibly and audibly. It was a sigh.

"Anyway," he said cordially. It *was* eleven in the morning, after all.

"You think a lot of yourself, but you're not sure you can handle this article about—what was it? Bookstores? Or maybe you could research Bobby Franco's sex life for us? That's much more our usual beat."

Yes, bookstores suddenly seemed terribly lame. Betty made fun of his inability to pass the most depressed storefront with a book in it.

"I mean I hope you can give me something personal here," she said.

"Well, that's what I was hoping, too." Thank you, Mr. Double-Entendre. Could we try the front door?

"No," she said, suddenly straightening up. He was hoping for another big inhalation, but she just loomed a little. "I meant that charming, roguish turn you have that character do in *London Bridge.*"

Then again, he could write a *genuinely* personal piece about bookstores and do it in his sleep. Books, he knew, had to do with his past. Visiting used bookshops, as he did quite compulsively, was like journeying in time from title to title. His mother's books, his father's books, books he had read on fall or spring Saturday mornings on the Seventy-ninth Street hill in Central Park opposite his father's Fifth Avenue apartment: *The Loneliness of the Long Distance Runner, Billy Liar*—that long-ago wave of British novelists...

"Oh, I know what I wanted to tell you," she said, pushing out from her chair.

"What?"

Now they were both standing, about to move somewhere. Most likely to the elevator. This was a busy lady.

"We're giving a little party for our new art director, Brian Brown, who did all the posters for us, you know?"

"Oh yes." The posters featured people looking over the shoulders of a child, or on occasion a rather nubile teenager, reading *Manhattan.* At the moment, they were all over the city.

"Anyway, it's from five to eight at the Palladium, and it'll be a—mix," she said with the smile on the last word. Now she stepped from behind her desk to lead him away.

"Great," he said, and followed. She had a nice, decorous ass, of a piece with the rest of her. But he was a little spoiled in that department. Betty's ass was sensational.

"I don't know just who, exactly, will be there," she said as they passed the watercooler and then walked through the glass doors into the elevator lobby. A black woman with diamante glasses pushed up over her hair sat behind the receptionist's desk.

"Anyway," Kate Warners said, "it would be fun to see you. And I hope you'll—"

An elevator door had opened and the lit-up red neon arrow on it pointed down.

"Oh, get that," she told him, "or you could be here for an hour."

"Okay," James said as he made for the elevator, "maybe I'll see you there."

"Great."

He stood in the middle of a large group in the elevator and looked at the editor. "Bye."

"Bye." She smiled.

He would have to wait till the door opened on the bottom floor to reclaim himself from the civilities cum abrupt impropriety of the preceding quarter of an hour. He seemed to be teetering over some abyss. To suddenly break ranks as he had was something he had silently toyed with but never before acted on. What was scary was that the act seemed all but involuntary. Betty and he were married, not unhappily as nearly as he could tell, so what was the source of so reckless an impulse? Then again, there was a violence in it that seemed to exceed any sexual element per se. Was he actively trying to subvert his success? That such behavior would be tolerated testified, perhaps, to his new ascendency, his personal power. But that was a bully's game, and a dangerous one. There was something to the fact, maybe, that everybody he was involved with professionally at the moment was a woman, that in fact they were his superiors. Was that at the bottom of the sudden hesitancy he'd felt to take the *Manhattan* assignment?

Out in the street once more, he was almost immediately walking beside the noisy, crowded playground of Robert F. Wagner Junior High School, which he'd attended for a term or two after P.S. 6 and before he went on to Trinity. This was the actual setting of his sexual awakening. It was here that puberty had first hit him, as if his life were suddenly going to take the shape of a rocket. Orin Clay, a cardiologist's son who was a classmate, had informed him one afternoon about masturbation. Four or five of them had been sitting around after school in Orin's room in his parent's Upper East Side townhouse and his schoolmates had made some remarks. When James expressed disbelief, Orin had taken up a girlie magazine and retired to the bathroom to re-emerge, approximately a minute and a half later, with his pants and underpants around his ankles and the white stuff on the end of his thirteen-year-old dick. It turned out they'd all been doing it three or four times a day; some restraint had held James to merely entertaining an erection at night in bed. That night, after Orin had demonstrated the strokes, James went ahead and repeated them until he could feel an upsurge inside himself that threatened the foundations of his world. His most immediate fear was that if he allowed himself Orin's release, the jet would shoot through the ceiling, bringing terrified tenants down from the floor above. He eased off his stroking, although the well of pleasure rising in him was almost too much to contain.

The following night he could no longer resist a release, even if it meant his being identified as a monster and taken away in shackles. To his relief, and slight disappointment, the issue of this premiere performance proved to be only mortal—sticky glop he hadn't properly prepared for and now needed to round up Kleenex to wipe up as best he could.

But the door had opened: like a door on the sky in the Salvador Dali painting; and he began *thinking* sexually, and almost immediately found spurs to his thought in the environment. Girlie magazines. Women on the street and, just now, as girls matured faster than boys, in the classroom. There was an audible gasp one day when a demure, rather tall thirteen-year-old named Mary Rosen stepped to the front of the class and walked in profile to the teacher's corner desk to pick up a paper as the male half of the class beheld her spectacular, and formerly unnoted, bosom. The poor girl darkened slightly, it seemed to James, in the subliminal charges of the moment.

Just what would be the proper attitude, given the rampant obsession with breasts just then, of a girl who found herself graced or cursed with such an endowment? Mary Rosen had had, as he remembered, a wry, rather grown-up way about her, although whether she'd be able to sustain that personal slant on things, or whether it would all be blasted away by her becoming a focus of adolescent furies, he didn't know. Those lives, the bodies and faces, were long gone, except via the random circuitry of his memory.

Was it memory itself, in fact, that comprised the real serendipity he was pursuing in these long, circuitous walks through New York? Was the city a kind of objective correlative of the intricate passage of the years, the numbered streets as in a dream interchangeable with the years of his life? Certainly the Wagner Junior High School playground brought him to that awakening he had known in 1959.

And to an older boy, name long forgotten, left back a few times so he was a classmate, with whom he had somehow begun to talk. He was a chunky kid, maybe fifteen to James's thirteen and more or less grown-up, who favored low slung jeans and had several white spots on each of his fingernails. Beyond that, he was into sex. He explained to James in study hall one day (a furiously windy, sunny-cold day outside rattling the windows so his lowered voice went unnoticed by Mr. Kolodny at his desk in front) what happened between a man and a woman:

"At night you find a nice private place in the park or somethin' and you sit down with a blanket maybe, you know? And you lie down and you take it out, see? And, see she's over you. See, she hasn't lied down. And she kinda hovers over it and goes back and forth, lookin' at the big thing and not lookin' at it. And then she starts—she gets curious, you know?—touchin' it. And then, pretty soon"—delivered in a cross between a shiver and a moan—"she's down on it."

Whether he was referring here to oral sex was lost on James, who was still in some confusion about the details of the more traditional practice, but the narrative proved unforgettable.

He also remembered this same boy being reprimanded in class by their math teacher, a tiny, heavily made up, ageless woman whose forehead had as many randomly intersecting lines as a roadmap, and who favored perfumes that could clear the sinuses. The boy reacted stoically, but then, when the teacher finished her reprimand and turned her back to him and continued up the aisle, he spray-spit through his teeth at her. The black jacket of her rayon suit was suddenly marked with a constellation of white dots of spittle, the flip side of his wad, as it were. James looked on, shocked to the roots of his scalp. The female authority figure—early variety.

He had walked to Fifth Avenue. Now he crossed the gridlocked midday traffic to the Central Park side and walked downtown toward his lunch appointment through the tree-dappled sunlight. Reva at the Russian Tea Room, a New York institution. The two of them were still really strangers; Reva had come in to write the deal with Annette Reed and Tri-Star when his previous agent, Sam McDowell, a model for one of the leads in *London Bridge,* had been asked to become a studio executive. He had decided to quit being an agent and take the offer.

4

Reva Makepeace was at her front table at the Russian Tea Room wearing something dark and silk, and he leaned over to kiss her cheek and then slid into the semicircular red leather booth opposite her. Reva's looks were a legend of the industry: a Eurasian Jewess with a lingering trace of a Bronx accent, she was just under six feet tall and her body had tautly supple, voluptuous contours that left James uneasy. She had had a seven-year marriage with no children, then divorced, and in two or three years evolved from an agent's secretary into a business powerhouse whose name on the phone was enough to cut through any studio executive's defense team of secretaries and assistants. She was rumored to have once lost her temper with a notoriously chauvinist gonzo journalist at a story meeting, and apparently would have beaten him badly if the others in the room hadn't held her back. Even his neighbor Henderson had heard a version of this story, though James had played dumb on the phone that morning.

"Hi!" Reva said, making her best effort at a sprightly agent-client rapport.

"Hi," he replied, smiling. "How are you?"

"I'm okay." Immediately switching into her lower, more sober octave, she added, "I've got some news."

"Oh?"

"Yeah, Annette called. She wants you out on the coast on Monday morning; you're gonna pitch *Success!* to Lindy Ramen at Fox."

"You mean the Valley girl?"

"Lindy? Listen, what do you feel like eating?"

A waiter had approached.

"Harry, how are you today?" Reva spoke directly and in a new tone to the white-haired, stooped old man in his red jacket. "Have you pulled yourself together?"

"Of course, Missus." Without looking at her, he made a perfunctory pass at their table with a red cloth napkin.

"Don't 'of course' *me,*" Reva suddenly spoke out loudly to him. "If I take care of you the way I do, I expect you to keep your wits about you and not get lost for a half an hour in the middle of the lunch. Do you understand, Harry?"

"Yes, Missus," he answered, looking up now but without looking directly at her, as though he had an astigmatism.

"Alright, Harry," she said in a quieter tone. "Don't go now. I want to order."

They studied menus for a moment, then ordered.

"Who told you Lindy was a Valley girl?"

"She did, at our last meeting, before she turned down *London Bridge*. Harvey Tilden, the producer who took the first option on it, kept getting distracted in his spiel by her—uh—bosom."

Reva smiled at him. She had a long face with high cheekbones, and a beautiful mouth with full sculptured lips. She was like an Aztec goddess, some immutably sorrowful strain pervading her features in vivid contrast to the here-today-gone-tomorrow ephemera that was the stuff of their business. James looked out into the brightly colored Old World gaiety of the restaurant. Across the room Michael Caine sat with his wife and a young blond woman, perhaps his daughter.

"Look, you think Lindy is stupid?"

"No."

"Well, don't fall into that trap that Hollywood sets for New York, okay? A twenty-four-year-old girl with big knockers who's screwing the boss has to be stupid? Wrong. Not well read, maybe; not a literary intellectual, maybe. But not stupid. Trust me on this one, James. Movies are movies, and that's something Lindy understands. Believe me, she understands that beautifully. She's behind two of the three hits they've got right now."

"I don't have a problem with her, or her—tits."

"Don't get funny." She paused here and studied him, as though she wasn't absolutely positive he deserved a set of keys to the executive washroom. "And do keep in mind that we're talking about Al Abbott's girlfriend, okay? That'll make it a lot easier for all of us."

Al Abbott was the head of 20th Century–Fox. "Look, I'm talking about Tilden, not me. I liked her. Sort of."

"Sort of." Reva kept smiling. "Listen, James, are you all right? Are you happy? How's your family? Uh..."

"Betty?"

"Betty, right. How's Betty?"

Family patter, more phony agent-client rapport. "I'm fine, Reva. But I think I'm going through some kind of crisis—now that you've made me such a big success."

"You are? Are you really? Okay, I'm glad you told me that. Do me a favor, though, will you?"

"Sure."

"Just try not to go crazy until you meet with Annette, okay? I'd like to get this movie squared away. I don't know—I think Lindy and Annette get along and this thing can fly if you just go out there and be the charming man I know you can be."

The old waiter put down a plate of smoked salmon and lemon in front of each of them and, after a few desultory passes at the table with his napkin, departed again.

"I didn't say I was going *crazy.*"

"*Everybody* goes crazy when they make it. Just try not to get the clap, will you? Not to mention...Oh, listen, speaking of crazy, guess who I ran into last night?"

"Who?"

"Allen Schweitzer—you know, Mr. Macho."

Allen Schweitzer was a moviemaking legend *inside* the business, since none of his movies had been a commercial success. Somehow or other, though, he had managed to write and direct four features backed by various studios. Each of them had a borderline psychotic hero, and a by-now trademark scene in which the hero consummated a sexual act standing up.

"Oh, yeah, the guy whose love scenes are all played vertically."

"Yeah, well I think Allen lives in absolute terror of the prone position," Reva said without smiling. "And he's just awful."

"Really?" James smiled. "I sort of like his movies. They're all about the fantasy life of us Upper East Side boys."

"I hope not—for Betty's sake. Anyway, I ran into him at Elaine's and he actually starts coming on to me, in front of a whole tableful of people and Elaine and everything. I mean like I'd been waiting my whole life to fuck the Harvard stallion, you know? Let me just say one thing, though."

Reva paused here, as if for dramatic emphasis, and gave him a smile that made the word *malevolent* pop up in his mind like toast.

"He's fucked in this business. And not just because of what he thinks he can get away with with me, although that doesn't help. I mean it's one thing to be a hustler, you know, but he's just *such* a scumbag."

James turned his head out toward the other tables. Had they heard this exchange? Was Reva speaking too loudly? He had no memory of Allen Schweitzer, though they'd both grown up on the Upper East Side and both gone to Harvard, but then James was a few years older than this auteur.

"So, did you go to bed with him?" he asked softly, smiling. This sort of intimacy was unusual between Reva and him.

"Did I go to bed with him? Did I go to bed with him? Listen, you *are* going crazy. *Please.* Oh, look, I don't even want to talk about it." She was obviously a little taken aback by the question. "But James, promise me you won't go nuts until after you get back from the coast, okay?"

It was important for him to remember that *everyone* was vulnerable. He knew that Reva and other women who now sat prominently at the helm of the movie industry had difficult love lives. Their professional manners were often preemptively forbidding, but by night they returned to empty apartments with old schoolbooks in the bookcase and a ratty teddy bear from their childhood bedroom. They commiserated with each other on the telephone after absurd dates on the same day they'd shepherded seven-figure contracts through the system. There was, at this time, it sometimes seemed to him, a sort of group sentiment among these females. Something to the effect that God had set the whole thing up to irritate one vice president in charge of packaging named Vicki (or Brenda; or Rosalyn). James could see and sympathize with the problem, but women of this stripe took him for married, and, at best, unlikely. And he *was* unlikely. But why was he also uncomfortable and somewhat insulted by the prevailing female power axis? Unfamiliarity? Certainly men were not lesser shits by any standard. But where the fuck *were* the men? They were, for the most part, hustling the same female power brokers as he. It was a switch.

*   *   *

After their lunch, he walked Reva to the corner of Sixth Avenue and Fifty-seventh Street, and they kissed good-bye.

"I'll have Ellen call you about the reservations."

"Okay. Thanks."

When she turned downtown toward her office, he continued walking east. It was still pale and sunny, now a little chillier. He was back among the anonymous horde, everybody unknown yet so stylish it was as if they were all somehow famous. New York fame—that kind of clarity of presence. And yet his actual one-on-one meetings with people seemed increasingly spectral. He walked on, somehow not very troubled. He had eaten a good lunch, and he had the slightly tranquilized sense of well-being that sometimes followed such meals.

Without being quite conscious of it, he took a route that brought him in ten minutes' time to the entrance of the Carlyle Bookstore on Fifty-eighth Street between Madison and Park. Therapy time. It was a venerable, older establishment with shelves and tables of dollar books outside the entrance, and first editions and prints inside. He opened the stained-glass paneled door and stepped into the store, accompanied by the tinkle of an attached bell. He began to browse along the floor-to-ceiling shelves, moving gradually toward the back.

At the end of the room, she sat at a desk talking on the telephone. He couldn't make out any of the words. She was simply another pretty woman, one he had noticed here once or twice before, inside the asylum of the shop, an opportunity for closer scrutiny than the street afforded. Casually, keeping his eyes on the books, he drew closer to the desk and then allowed himself another brief glance as he stood about midway in the store and surveyed the print gallery beyond her desk, a few steps up from the ground level at the back. The prints were of no interest to him.

In fact, she was more than pretty, a beauty of a darker hue than, say, Betty, and with a full figure—her breasts looked quite heavy in her dark blouse—and now there was a sudden fullness in the pit of his throat.

He decided to go downstairs to look at the fiction in the basement. She hung up the phone after he passed her desk, which sat just in front of the stairway to the basement. As he began walking down the stairs, he realized he was heading into pitch darkness and turned back.

"Is the basement open today?" he asked her from behind.

She turned and looked at him from her chair. She had long black hair, and a kind of languorous cast to her face with just a trace of a smile. She was a woman to find on a stretch of beach in the South Sea Islands. She would change your life forever.

"Oh, yes," she answered. "It's just the light. It's right at the bottom of the stairs."

"Thanks," he said smiling, switching from Paul Gauguin back to Mr. Lucky.

"Sure," she answered with the tiniest twinkle back. "If you can't find it, just give a scream."

A scream? She meant a holler. But he liked the easy tone she was practicing. Book lovers' rapport—knock off the "book" part and the electrical currents might be recordbreaking. She was maybe in her mid to late twenties, New York vowels. "Okay," he said and took the stairs carefully. Major accident like falling down the stairs to be avoided. Don't want to start off on the wrong foot.

At the bottom of the stairs, he found the light and switched it on but for all he knew the entire basement stock might have been made up of thousands of copies of one title—say, the orange covered one, *The Tents of Wickedness* by Peter De Vries. Not that he was particularly sexually excited, but rather his entire central nervous system was inside some kind of radiant shower. Eros, after all, was an important part of the creative impulse: the same juices that made a play or a screenplay made a love play.

As he wandered through the two drab gray parallel corridors, he tried to remember, as best he could, her contours. It was impossible, like trying to remember a painting by de Kooning. The point was that she made the air get thick, and his throat thicken with that combination of excitement and sadness.

Sometimes, it was true, you just looked and you knew. Your eyes translated a woman's look and her form into some absolute of rapport and license. The way the bridge of the nose joined the brow could promise a pride of arching back and buttocks. At the same time, given a naturally romantic bent, James needed to bring himself up short. During the first year of his life, his father had been in London in the army, and he wondered if he hadn't known in earliest childhood a precocious awakening. His mother had been beautiful then and scarcely more than a girl, and part of his adolescent reticence might have had to do with the Dionysian tumult he knew at his core. Betty had been significantly, if only very briefly, first a *friend,* which helped to ground him when he discovered her physical charms were close to his ideal. Yet that ideal itself may have involved a rational one-remove from the heavier essence one sensed in the woman upstairs. This, given her look, could lead him right over the precipice he had spent his adulthood keeping properly demarcated.

But it all *was* lust, of course. Though that hadn't meant much to him, ever, because lust, as far as he was concerned, was inextricably tied up with trust. He was no rapist, not one who enjoyed humiliating an unwilling partner. His fantasy was losing control, pure and simple, in the throes of overwhelming attraction. It was a terrible fantasy, but what were you supposed to do?

So he walked back up the stairs, passed her at her desk without so much as a look and walked the length of the shop and back out the stained-glass paneled door (ding-a-ling) and out onto the street again. The dull roar of New York—bodies hurrying, hurrying, hurrying. He couldn't see a thing and paused several feet east of the shop to take stock. The point was not just that he wanted to *fuck.* But what if it *was?* So what?

Let's take another look, friend, before we put ourselves to sleep with quandariness. He walked the few steps back and entered the shop again and caught a glimpse of her face at the end of the room. The immediate answer didn't come in words, but rather again his whole being took her in like some kind of benediction: the sun on water. She was beauty in the world, the same world he was in, at the same time. By an amazing, God-given coincidence, they shared this very room.

The miracle on Fifty-eighth Street.

"Do you have anything by William Maxwell?" He had walked to her desk, catching her eye for the last few strides.

"I just *had* a first of *The Folded Leaf*. Really nice condition. But I'm afraid it's gone." She gave him a sympathetic, little mock-tearful smile.

"What about Daniel Fuchs's Williamsburg series? Do you ever get any of those in?"

"Oh, those are really rare. I don't think they printed a lot, you know, in the first edition. And they go like *that*."

They traded more book gossip, while he kept his eyes casual, moving over her eyes, her face and hair, into the room at large, various customers with packages and pocketbooks. His heart was beating swiftly now, and he took in the rest of her only peripherally. He was talking with her; he had broken through some invisible membrane into another neighborhood of experience. For the second time today, he had broken his own rules.

"Listen," he said, searching for a shift to give further impetus to the conversation, "maybe you could help me with something. I'm a writer..."

"Really—published?" she answered immediately.

"Well, produced actually. I'm a screenwriter."

"Oh. Anything I might know?"

"Well, you might. I wrote *London Bridge*... It's playing now."

"Oh, of course. I saw it. I liked it. A *lot*." She looked at him differently, he thought, just then.

Fame, after all, had arrived to provide him larger access in the world. His art might even benefit. His heart might broaden. Here was a flower of the streets, you might say, a home-grown queen of the island working her way up through the ranks. She had typing skills. Reception skills. Reception skills? On the other hand, maybe he was going nuts.

"Thank you," he answered.

"And wasn't there something about you in the Sunday *Times* a while ago?"

There had been a feature the Sunday preceding the movie's New York premiere that focused on Annette and him, but he was surprised that anyone not in the business would remember it. "You've got a good memory."

"Well... I like films. Is it—Redding?" she asked hesitantly. She seemed for the moment unstrung, vulnerable.

"Right. Jamie Redding. But anyway, I may be writing a piece for *Manhattan* about New York specialty bookstores, and of course I'd want to cover the Carlyle."

"Great." Now she was all but beaming at him. Even so, her nature didn't seem ebullient, but rather softer, darker, riper. The tension in her personality was between this gravity-bound essence, and her own will to be day-bright, professional, "on." It was sexy.

"I'm supposed to be downtown this evening, but

would it be possible to call you and we could talk about the shop?"

"You mean here?"

"Sure, or I could buy you a drink."

"Well, we close at five thirty."

He moved from beside her desk and glanced over titles in the belles lettres section that was nearest along the wall. Nigel Nicolson's memoir of his parents, *A Portrait of a Marriage.* Betty had a gardening book by his mother, Vita Sackville-West. The Bloomsbury gardeners. Everybody up to their elbows in dirt, flowers, neuroses, war, genius, Keynesianism, homosexuality, abscesses, idealism, talent, feminism. He looked back at her. She was writing a number on a piece of paper. She held it up to him.

"I'm usually at home by six."

He wasn't about to argue. "Great," he said, and took the piece of paper, which was pad-sized with a Carlyle letterhead.

"Or you can reach me here from ten thirty on, Monday through Friday."

The piece of paper had a number, but no name. "Oh, but I don't know your name."

She stood up now and, as he held it forward, took the piece of paper again. "Sorry, it's Joan," she said. She was a little shorter than Betty, maybe five foot five. She had a very good figure which her dark blouse and skirt rather played down. It was a style he liked, let's make it our little secret, or at least not play it for all it's worth to the public at large. "Joan Wallin."

He took the piece of paper back from her. It was

time to go now, counting his many blessings. "I'll call you then, as soon as I get squared away. Nice to meet you. Oh, and I'll take the book."

She had shown him a copy of the small second printing of Henry Roth's *Call It Sleep* with a very good dust jacket. It was two hundred dollars, and he paid for it with his American Express card. It was an absurd purchase; he wasn't a book collector. He bought to read, and prided himself on his bargains. He said good-bye again and left with the book in a white Carlyle bag under his arm.

Walking at sundown through the Murray Hill district on Third Avenue (he had stopped for a cappuccino and at two more bookshops to while away the rest of the afternoon), gradually heading toward the Palladium, he rehearsed their conversation and her apparent readiness to admit him to the nonprofessional precincts of her life. Why? He knew he wasn't the greatest looking man she could find. It was his success, of course. But then it was funny about beautiful women. When he'd met Betty she had come to New York directly after graduating from Bennington and was about to move in with a gay sculptor who needed help with his rent. Instead, a day or two after they met, she and James rented a studio apartment in Yorktown and he moved out of the Upper West Side apartment he shared with another writer. And she had had, by this time, her share of romances.

"Did you fuck him?" he would ask, when some new name would crop up in the conversation.

"I can't remember," she actually answered on occasion.

"Sure, you can't remember whether you fucked him." Once, he had come up with an impersonation of her as Little Red Riding Hood talking to her psychiatrist in a tiny little voice: "I went to the eye-doctor, doctor, and we tried a few lenses and he put his hand on my shoulder, my knee, my back, my bottom, my ear, and my breast—but only very quickly on each of them so I knew he wasn't making a pass at me, but it was just his manner."

"I see," the psychiatrist answered in a thick German accent James contrived. "And vot vas he vearing?"

"Oh, just these cute little black bikini underpants."

Betty laughed and protested, and in fact she was no longer the sixties blonde *naïve* she had been. But the erotic life of a beautiful woman would make a very interesting—what? Porno film? The porno films he'd seen on cable—where they left everything showing except the men's genitals, a complicated sexism he'd never sorted out—had the herky-jerky, patently unsexy accelerations of silent movies. Everything happened too fast, and too mindlessly.

He found a telephone on the corner of Twenty-seventh and Third Avenue and pressed all his credit card digits.

"Hello."

"Hi."

"James, how are you?"

"Fine, fine. But Reva says I'm gonna have to be out on the coast by Monday morning for a few days."

"I know. Ellen called a little while ago with the reservations. I've got everything written down."

"Thanks, honey. And, oh, listen, the editor at *Manhattan* invited me to this cocktail party at Palladium..."

"Lucky you."

"Yeah, well, we'll end up there again soon, but I thought I should go and mix, you know."

"Of course. Go and mix."

"But the thing is—if it gets late, I should probably wait till tomorrow to drive home." It came out like clockwork. For a moment it was as if he caught his own image in a mirror without recognizing it. "I'll crash at the Essex House and then drive home tomorrow."

"Okay, I hope you're having a great affair."

"What?" He was loudly incredulous.

"Just kidding. Oh, but do you want to hear that man speak at the high school tomorrow?"

"Oh, right. How's Lisa?"

"She's in her room watching a *Little House on the Prairie* rerun."

He turned around and saw that a middle-aged woman in a pea jacket and jeans was standing beside the corner building looking at him, waiting; he turned back and faced the phone again. A woman in a pea jacket looking slightly peeved. A lesbian most likely. Women were in trouble. So was he.

"Well, we're going to have to give her an ultimatum; either she phones one of her classmates or you and I go to see Mrs. what's-her-name, the counselor."

"Mrs. Smathers? I just thought that maybe it would help to hear whatever this shrink has to say first."

"Yeah, I do too. I'll be home for it. I may come home tonight. What time is it again?"

"At three at the high school."

"How's everybody else?"

"We're fine."

"Okay, honey. I love you."

"I love you."

He hung up the phone and crossed the street and continued walking downtown. The sun was beginning to go down.

5

The enormous bouncer at the entrance of the Palladium had a list with his name on it. He was duly admitted to Steve Rubell's class system. Upstairs, downstairs. But instead of British aristocracy above, you had Andy Warhol and Keith Haring. Inside, he walked to the room at the far end of the main floor, and gave his name again. He was admitted to a room so crowded it was like a single amorphous organism. Encompassed, he aimed at the bar. Under the pounding new wave beat, there were also voices. He recognized the piercing octave of Rene Swift, an early Warhol star, an Aubrey Beardsley lookalike who was a fair poet and a legendary talker.

"My solution," he was telling someone, or some part of someone, "is to kidnap James Atlas and demand the immediate resignation of Norman Podhoretz and Hilton Kramer. It's time to blow the whistle on the neoliberal, neoconservative riffraff, darling. I will appear at the ransom negotiations with a stocking over my face and a copy of *Mother Jones*."

The old guy was still cooking. He might have said hello but he was sure Rene wouldn't recognize him and with the crush of bodies and voices, plus that beat blasting over, around, and through him, it would be an exhausting encounter. Instead he kept on his course toward the bar, clutching his book under his arm.

Further on, he heard a man's rich, slurred voice say: "Diane Arbus was sick, but Weegee, on the other hand, was a vigorous urban primitive, and his work retains love's life-giving vulgarity."

"Frank O'Hara," he said out loud to no one in particular.

"I beg your pardon?"

He looked to his left and discovered Michael Roberts, another sixties acquaintance, now an art critic. "Hi. Jamie Redding."

"I know. Why did you say Frank's name like that?"

"Because somebody just plagiarized 'love's life-giving vulgarity' to put down Diane Arbus. Frank wouldn't have liked that."

Michael Roberts, a Midwesterner who had been slight and agile, had, in the years since James had last seen him, filled out. He looked surprisingly formidable now. "Well," he said, holding his drink and looking at James with an indulgent smile, "I know you like Diane Arbus now. What else is new?"

"You tell me—*Miami Vice?*" he answered smiling. "I better get a drink."

"Sure," Roberts said. "What are you doing here?"

"I'm having a wonderful time, Mike. How about you?"

"Redding," Roberts called to him as he broke through, in a sudden shift of bodies, to within an arm's reach of the bar, "I think you've changed. You've lost your innocence."

"Thanks, Michael," he called back, still facing him, smiling.

Roberts made no further comment and his eyes seemed distracted. When James got to the bar and ordered a Heineken he realized that Joan Wallin would be home now, doing whatever she did when she got home. Did she live with a man? It was hard to believe anyone that good-looking could be living alone, but they said the naked city had a million stories.

His first sip of beer was a great pleasure—like a lit window in the night. He debated asking the female bartender, a leather-clad punker with a Joan Jett haircut, if he could stash the book in back of the counter, but he could see the wet dust jacket at the evening's end and his guilt would be compounded. What was he doing spending money like that? Even if he now had it to spend?

He unbuttoned his shirt and put the book package in between his T-shirt and his shirt and buttoned it again. Now he could hold his drink and see if he could move.

Roberts was almost immediately before him again.

"I want to add to what I began. We're all surprised at what's happened to you. We thought you were committed to the same things we were, that we were all in consensus..."

"Is this the royal or the editorial *we?*" James interrupted.

"Pardon?" Roberts said.

"Michael, you drunk?"

"No, or if I am, it's none of your business, you

goddamn capitalist!" He smiled here to let James know this was all just pomp and circumstance, not to be taken to heart or into gut. As if that were even a remote possibility. Paying dues dissolved guilt; Roberts wouldn't get too quickly under his skin. He decided to switch subjects.

"Hey, Mike, is it my imagination or did we do this all before in the sixties?" he said, indicating as best he could the room at large.

Roberts hesitated. "Well," he said finally, "I think they're getting it right this time."

"Why? Because it costs eighteen dollars for girls from Queens to get in here, if they're good-looking enough *to* get in?"

"Look at it this way: If the West has got to go down, this is the way it should go."

He let it ride, turning away from Roberts with a slight smile. He would really like to take a bath with Joan Wallin. This room was too full of show business. He wanted a room with the specifics of a personal life littering it: somebody's little comb, the smell of a mildewed paperback. The way to success in New York was to eliminate one's personal life, and/or to make it entirely public. Andy Warhol, whom he'd just caught a glimpse of in the room's corner, was the prototype. He was everywhere a flashbulb went off: he was photographed and the photographs were printed everywhere.

Joan Wallin and her first editions, her shoes, her hair. He might call her up and see if he could get invited over to her apartment. It would be a tiny walk-up somewhere, a find. It would have a history, personal and sexual, old stories running through its walls and floorboards. Here was Kate Warners, though, looking svelte in a sleeveless black sheath.

"Kate?"

"Oh, hi! You *came.* How are you? I'm excited about your piece. I mean whatever it's going to be."

"I figured it out," he said, smiling at her. "I'm going to do *adult* bookstores." Why did he have this compulsion to ruffle this lady's always nicely composed feathers?

"Hmmm." She paused now, averting her eyes into the surrounding chaos. "So we're still the little boy..."

"Hey, this could be big. I was thinking I could go underground on Times Square—peep shows, massage parlors, fetishes, golden showers, the whole sewer system. You know, a really groundbreaking piece."

She observed him levelly. "You know you really are sick or something. How 'bout you just shut up and dance?"

"Dance?"

"They've opened the dance floor. Do you dance?"

"Sure."

"It's through here, just follow me."

She turned and began moving toward the corner entrance, trailing a white hand behind her, which he took gently with his hand. But how did it happen she was already calling the shots? The little black dress, the little white girl inside it, her little Seven Sisters education—and he wasn't even the gamekeeper anymore. Just a goddamn aerobic accessory. Time to trip the light fantastic...

* * *

They passed through the corner entrance and exit and made a sharp right onto the Palladium's central dance floor, already full of dancing bodies. Kate and he made their way into the mélange and began moving to the beat. There wasn't room, spatially or melodically, for anything very subtle, but all of them couldn't miss keeping time. He smiled at Kate, who smiled back, and they continued their moves without looking into each other's eyes. It was oddly cozy, despite the decibels, all of them rhythmically subsumed, and soon enough sweating into the bargain.

He let his body shake away some of the accumulated accents of the day, noticing now for the first time his exhaustion. He was conscious of his book under his shirt, and then it seemed there was too little oxygen in the room.

A little "ah" went up from the surrounding crowd and he looked up as a rectangular backdrop was lowered to the floor on pulleys from the domed ceiling above. This was the old Academy of Music, an opera house in the 1800s. The change of backdrop was the work of a New York painter, though just whom he couldn't say. It was brightly painted, double-exposed realism, hard to see.

Now the number began to end and he put some last-minute reserves into finishing with honor. Kate looked at him as if to say "Again?" and he said out loud, "I think I'm dead."

"You're dead already? Get this man to Jack LaLanne!"

Hahaha. "Yeah, well," he answered, "this is just *too* goddamn exciting. The next thing you know Steve

Rubell's gonna walk in here and I'm going to have a heart attack."

"You're so bitter. Why? You're a success now. Where are you from?"

"Tijuana."

"Very funny. It shows."

"Are you staying over?" she asked him more pleasantly when they were back inside the party room. "Or going back to Connecticut tonight?"

"I think I'm heading back," he answered, smiling.

She was seemingly unattached, and apparently available for an evening's adventures, but he didn't want to get involved with her. She was too social, too important, too intelligent, too happy about the world, too New York, New York, the Bronx is up, the Battery's down. In any case, his own battery was running down now: he was losing the day's raw momentum and fading back into his perennial mental traffic: guilt, apprehension of disaster, fear of flying. He would catch her later maybe. Someone had said: When you're young you're afraid you'll miss the boat; but when you get older, you realize the boat comes all the time. It was the sort of maxim that comforted now that one of his wisdom teeth had commenced its familiar dull ache. That meant he was into his reserves.

"So you're all bark and no bite."

"I don't mean to let you down, Kate."

"What's your problem, then, huh? I mean you come up to my office and spout this filth. I think you're sick. Just go fuck yourself, okay?" she said, beginning a passage back into the main room.

For the first time, he felt stung and sobered by her anger, which had the unimpeachable dignity of authentic emotion. Yet the idea of a woman finding his behavior so degrading implied a terrible yawning gulf between them that saddened him. He realized he would probably be the subject of a female executive's commiserating phone call.

In the darkness of the Mercedes, cruising along the West Side Highway with the George Washington Bridge up ahead like a green jeweled brocade across the night, he was almost ready to turn back and call Joan Wallin and undertake major designs. But Reva had asked him to wait for the movie deal to get squared away first, and anyway a call tonight might smack of desperation.

He fiddled with his radio dial and found the "*WPIX Penthouse*" with DeBarge, who sounded like a woman, singing "All This Love Waiting for You." When DeBarge went off, a spurious crossover jazz took over, and he switched off the radio. He wished he had a cassette of Ellington's *Jazz Violin Sessions,* but since he didn't he kept the car quiet, purring through the night.

He remembered drives at sunset from West Marin up into Sonoma County to the repertory movie house in Petaluma where he caught up on some of the films they'd missed since they'd had babies. Betty usually stayed home. He drove their old Volvo by fields of black-and-white cows in the deepening darkness. He could smell the dairyland in the car: a curiously soothing smell made up of earth, grasses and cow dung. The black of the cows' bodies had already blended into the night. Only the white fragments of cows remained visible along the road. Or was that a literary flight of fancy?

He was too tired to figure it out. Driving, he moved his neck and shouted: "Hello. Joan Wallin? Jamie Redding. You're beautiful. I'd like to come over and talk. Later we could make love. After I sleep for fifty hours..." He kept his eyes studiously on the road. It wasn't a country road with cows, but a turnpike with lit-up gas stations, turnoffs and rest stops.

The movie house was called the Petaluma Plaza and the crowd was remarkably similar to the sort he remembered at the Bleecker Street Cinema in the early sixties. A hard-core film crowd made up, he knew, of more than a few transplanted Easterners, now out there in cowtown. He had seen Bertolucci's *1900* there one night in a packed house, and gotten up from his seat with awe at so huge an achievement, and wonder that it had made so little impact in America. A few years later, at dinner with Harvey and Martha Tilden in the hills of West Hollywood, he had gotten the dirty lowdown. Tilden had once optioned *London Bridge* but hadn't been able to put a deal together.

"You know," he said to James with a smile, "MGM gave Bertolucci millions of dollars for that movie before they realized he was a Communist."

But the Petaluma crowd was a big, fervent one and they applauded at the end, the ultimate accolade. Communist or not—it hadn't even entered his mind while he watched the movie—Bertolucci had made it into the American heartland, the dairy country, also infiltrated by ex-New Yorkers, some of them now wearing cowboy hats.

Now on the Saw Mill, the road had darkened, with fewer signs and turnoffs, but it wasn't anything to compare to Sonoma's pastureland spread out under the stars with farmhouses set far back from the road. So many Easterners had moved out there, some of them bringing an influx of energy and savvy into the town. In a way, it was all a part of the cowboy syndrome. Ivy League graduates playing John Wayne. James himself had actually worn a knife in its holster strapped on his belt for a week or two. For a while, too, his best friend was a young Vietnam vet from Novato, a tree surgeon named Ray Ebert who frequently turned his back during outdoor conversation to unzip his pants and piss, as a sign, James understood, of implicit masculine command. Ray Ebert and he had been "brothers" for a while, but James had been going in another direction; that glorious, glad, go-power of youth was waning in him and his deeper resources had nothing to do with riding his edge. That edge might give a play a compelling formal dynamic, but it seemed by definition an emotional narrows. He was in need of continuing and deepening his education, mostly by reading and writing and being a husband and father, until his capacity for sympathy, for a playwright's spectrum of empathic identification, enlarged. The macho thing was like a last-minute bonus of his youth but he had only the briefest moment in that particular sun. He had been college-deferred and then a psychiatric 4-F (prompted by a letter from a psychiatrist and family friend who characterized him to the draft board as "temperamentally unfit" and liable to be unbalanced by the army's authority structure). He'd never given Vietnam a chance. Ray Ebert, on the other hand, had gone the distance with a crack combat unit and now liked to read the *Federalist Papers* by kerosene oil lamp at night in his cabin after work.

But there was something irretrievably strained and silly about Harvard boys trying to impersonate the "yep" and "nope" crowd; and the old-timers, the natives, were none too thrilled by these youngsters, who frequently displaced them as the town officials and set up building moratoriums and fought the county government for self-determination. In their own little town, people had gotten around growth control by building substandard second units and renting them out. The population had thereby doubled without any significant boost of the tax base. Some of the most vociferous of the New York axis were chastened.

But seeing their old New York friends again, the ones who hadn't left, or sometimes even changed apartments, had also been chastening. It was as if during the interim of a decade they had made trips to the grocery store and the laundromat and attended a lot of parties. In essence, they were the same people but ten years older, tireder, more entrenched, their neuroses thickened into routine. One old friend, Edward Vox, a magazine journalist who had been working on a novel for years and the model for another of the characters in *London Bridge,* had even told Betty and him that he was afraid to date anymore.

"And I'm not queer, man, you know? But I mean I know people who've got AIDS, and some of them and other people know people who have *died* of it. And it's just really, really scary."

He put the Mercedes into the garage, took his book and got out and walked out of the garage and onto the stone courtyard. The night was quite chilly and the sky was full of stars. He stood for a moment looking up and listening to the silence of the neighborhood, so resonant after New York. Then he went into the house. The kitchen clock read ten-fifty. He went upstairs and caught a glimpse of Betty in her dark blue Pierre Deux robe with the kids, also dressed for bed, all on their big bed watching Friday night television. He went into the bathroom and checked himself in the mirror. He looked curiously the same. He took two five-hundred-milligram calcium-magnesium tablets for his wisdom tooth, and went into their bedroom.

"Hi," Betty said, smiling up from *Miami Vice* with the rosy flush she sometimes had at night. "You came home."

"Yeah, the party was pretty dull," he said and, as casually as possible, took the book out of the bag and laid it on their night table. As far as he knew there was no price marked in it. He dropped the Carlyle bag into their wastebasket beside the bureau.

Paul, at the far end of the bed in his white thermal pajamas, was alseep. Stephanie, next to him and wearing her flannel nightgown, looked up at James, smiled, and then looked back at the television. Lisa, in her pink flannel nightgown, looking not appreciably smaller than her mother, was studiously absorbed by Crockett and Tubbs and the pastel harmonies of a *Miami Vice* art deco interior. She didn't look up.

He left the room and went into Paul's room and pulled down his bed covers so that he could carry him in to his bed, glancing reflexively up at Michael Jackson's clown face on the calendar over the bed. Michael Jackson was a kind of angel to the very young, James had realized one night recently, tucking Paul into bed after one of his first days back at school; he was someone they could call on for help in their dreams. James returned to their bedroom and reached across the bed to his son's curled-up body and lifted him.

While being carried to his room, Paul, with his eyes still closed, struggled in his arms and said, "No, no, Dad...no, no...no, no, no..."

James laid him gently down and his son seemed to surrender back into sleep, his protests subsided. He covered him, switched off the light, and returned to their bedroom.

There were people hiding behind palm trees, and a killer in a white linen suit stalking them. A little boy was behind one tree. Then, just at the moment it looked like everything was over for the innocent, Crockett and Tubbs pulled up in the black Ferrari and aimed their .38s.

"Surf's up, pal," Crockett said in the gravely voice that complemented so nicely his smooth blond good looks. The guy turned, fired, and Sonny shot him and he fell.

They cut to a scene with the lieutenant and ended with Crockett's smile, his multimillion-dollar smile. He had known guys like Don Johnson in California—not as handsome maybe, and not as smart, but the same type: good old boys.

"You should write something for him," Betty said when the commercial came on and she switched the sound off.

"Sure," he said, "me and every other writer in America."

"But he's a *good* actor," Betty insisted.

"Right," he said, smiling. "I can tell you like his acting a lot."

"Dad," Lisa said, looking up for the first time, "Mom is so in love with Don Johnson it's pathetic."

"I am *not,*" Betty said, seriously. "I think he's cute, but he really *is* a good actor and you don't see that on TV that much."

"Sure," James said; and then, addressing Lisa and Stephanie, "Okay, you guys, surf's up."

"Nice try, Dad," Stephanie said, giggling and getting up from the bed. "Nice try, *but*..."

Sometime after midnight, he woke up hearing someone wheezing and coughing and Betty rushed out of their bed. Several minutes later, she was back.

"What was that?" he said after she'd gotten back into bed.

"Stephanie. She came home with a cough, but I don't know *what* this was. It was like she couldn't breath—like asthma or the croup. And then she had a big burp and it was okay. It got cold all of a sudden tonight, so I turned up the heat."

"Good. Is she upset or something? She's never had asthma."

"Of course she's upset. This is her third school in a year, and it's junior high. It's bigger and they're changing classes every period, and she's a preteen, which is worse than being a teenager I think."

"What does she say?"

"Nothing, but she talked for about an hour on the phone with some girl named Laura, just incredible girl gossip about nothing for over an hour."

"That's good, isn't it?"

"Yes, except she's very nervous."

She had closed her eyes. He took the Itty-Bitty Book Lite from his side of the bed and read three or four pages of *Call It Sleep* before he could feel gravity on his eyes again, and he put the book back on the bed table and switched off the light.

6

Sitting with Betty in the high school auditorium in an audience of concerned parents listening to the psychologist, a middle-aged, balding man named Fingeroth, talk about the trials of adolescence, James found himself periodically losing the thread of the talk in half-conscious reverie on Joan Wallin. In secret, he now carried this radiant and tumultuous center inside him. What could be wrong with his life for him to be doing this? But the question was a rhetorical gesture. He was happy in his reverie, full of romantic currents of sadness and happiness.

"In twenty-four hours, I sometimes don't have the time to have a decent five-minute conversation with my daughter," Dr. Fingeroth told them all rather buoyantly. "And what do I do about it? I feel guilty as hell, that's what I do about it. And, if I feel guilty enough about it, I squeeze the time in at the last minute, too."

It seemed to have only marginal relevance to Betty and him, and rather to be directed to upwardly mobile superachievers who, in their climb up the corporate beanpole, had perhaps stepped upon the psyches of their growing children. Yet he had no right, he knew, to feel anything but sympathy and concern for everyone there. After the amusing talk, there was a question period.

"What do you do when you see your child isn't trying?" a man in a white cardigan with prematurely white hair had stood up to ask.

The answer involved a number of options, depending on the severity of the child's defection from the standards of the parents, from cancellation of allowance, to grounding, to the engagement of professional help. James knew his own sympathy for the child was mostly sentimental, and that in his own house he might one day soon have to face down teenage mutiny.

As they were heading for their car in the parking lot in the mild, sunny Saturday afternoon, Betty remarked, "I felt like leaving in the middle. It was like we were all there to assuage *his* guilt."

"Yeah," James answered, getting in on the passenger side of her blue Volvo wagon, "and not one word about, you know, having a family is an interesting experience, or fun, or rewarding."

"Of course not," Betty said, getting into the driver's seat and slamming the door. "He's having a much better time lecturing us than talking to his—"

"His *one* child," James broke in. "He doesn't even have a family. Take it from me, being an only child is a lot different from being in a larger family."

Betty had pulled the car out of the parking space and was driving slowly through the parking lot as other parents moved through it on their way to their cars. She had a sister, but not a brother, which she'd always wanted.

"Well," she said, "ready to move back to the barn in Septic City and hang out with the California dropouts for a few more decades?"

"I didn't mean that," he said, looking at the slow-moving, somehow burdened posture of a man in red and white checked pants opening the door to his wine-red BMW. "These people are touching in their own ways. I know that. And California is over for me."

"Good!" Betty said and smiled at him from the wheel.

He liked it when she drove.

Later that afternoon, he found the door to Lisa's room locked. He knocked.

"Who is it?"

"It's me."

"I don't want to talk about it."

"Open the door, Lisa."

"I'm taking a nap."

"Lisa, open the door or there's no television tonight."

He could hear her get off her bed, and then her heavy footfalls. The door opened. She was dressed in jeans and a blue sweatshirt.

"Thank you," he said, smiling and stepping into the room. He closed the door behind him.

"Oh no," she said, "I can see this is going to be a big deal, right?"

"Lisa, just sit down and let's talk about things, all right?"

She sighed and sat down on her bed while he took the wood chair with the rush seat in the middle of the room. The yellow maple stirred at the second-floor picture window like a benevolent watchdog.

"Here's the situation. Betty and I have talked it over and we realize that you're making this into a big problem when really it's—"

Lisa stood up and shouted, "No, I'm not!"

"Not what?" he said, startled.

"Not making it into a big problem!"

He heard a tremendous thud outside her door.

"Paul?" he shouted, remaining in his chair.

"Yes," his son answered in an even tone on the other side of the door.

"Don't *run* and don't *jump*—I've told you that now five times today; if I have to say it again there's no TV tonight."

"Sorry, Dad," he said. "I'm just getting my mit. Mark and I are going to play catch."

"Great," he called out to him.

"Dad?" he said.

"Yes."

"Would you play catch with us?"

"Not right now, Paul. I'm talking with Lisa."

"Maybe later, then?"

"We'll see."

"Okay, Dad. Thanks." The thanks, he knew, was part of Paul's strategy to get him out on the lawn.

He turned back to his daughter. She was sitting on her bed again. In better times, they shared a similar taste in music and he liked her sense of humor.

He had spent enjoyable evenings in the living room with a book while she did her homework and monitored the turntable. She liked Marvin Gaye and he'd discovered that he liked Talking Heads and UB40. "It's really very simple," he said.

"No, it isn't. You think it is because you have all your friends here from before but I don't and you don't care about me. All you care about is your little boy."

"That's ridiculous."

"Just get out of here!" She was suddenly standing up again yelling and at the same time there were tears in her eyes.

He stood up, catching sight of an issue of *Rolling Stone* with Don Johnson on the cover under her bed. "Look, Lisa, I'm going to make this very simple. You have till the end of the month to call somebody, I don't care who. Now, if you don't do that, we're going to have to talk with the counselor at school, Mrs. Smathers."

"*Nooo!*" she shrieked in an ear-splitting roar worthy of Medea.

He didn't need to yell back. "And I don't care if nothing comes of it," he backpedaled.

"I hate you! You *fucker!*" she yelled.

"Shut up!" he yelled back, leaving.

"*I hate you so much,*" she told him now with her mouth clenched, each word a dagger.

He opened her door and walked out of her room and closed the door behind him.

"*Fucker!*" she roared again at the top of her lungs as he was going downstairs.

A little chat with his adolescent daughter. What was

going on? Primal scream therapy? This sure as hell never happened on *The Cosby Show.*

In the fall twilight, he and Paul and Mark threw the baseball back and forth. Mark was a little smaller than Paul and obviously a natural athlete. James had wondered if the boy's hands were quite big enough to grip the ball, and here he was pegging his throws in as if accuracy were second nature.

Paul, though also well coordinated, was more ruminative in his style, holding the ball for a moment to establish who would throw to whom, and how long James would stay in their game.

"Till it gets dark, Dad?"

It was already darkening. "I don't know, Paul, but let's just enjoy what we're doing now and not do a lot of planning, okay?"

Things would grow quiet again and the game of catch take mindless precedence for a while. A long throw of Paul's had James running for all he was worth and then, Willie Mays style, managing a basket catch.

"Good one, Dad."

He threw it over to Mark who stuck his glove in the air as if he were half-asleep and snagged it. He was a scruffy little boy with red hair and freckles. He and Paul spent a lot of time wrestling. It was a pleasure to see Paul becoming, in the past year or so and despite the move, so much more physically self-contained and centered. These were important years, he knew, when the whole personality could coalesce, and that seemed to be what was happening with Paul. On the other hand, James remembered when he had been eight and his parents divorced: for the next year or so he had been thrown into a sort of twilight zone of disorientation, finding it hard to study, to play, or to do very nearly anything at all. He had been zonked, and was suddenly living with his mother alone and going to Greenwich Country Day School, which proved to be more difficult than P.S. 6.

"So," he said to both boys, "what do you think about Mr. Watson? Is he a good teacher?"

"He's a good teacher," Mark said to him seriously, nodding, and then smiled, revealing an absent front tooth.

James got the impression the boy had given him the answer he figured he wanted to hear. The teacher was reputed to be a severe disciplinarian; Paul had regaled them with stories of his yelling, breaking pencils, even tipping over desks, but James hadn't yet discerned how much of this had actually happened and how much of it was school legend.

"But did he ever break your pencil?" he asked his son's friend. Break a pencil? Was this serious? This was no California me-decade school, that was clear. Break a child's pencil in a Marin County school, and you'd probably be looking at a legal proceeding. Suspension maybe. A prison term?

"No, but he yelled at me," Mark answered.

"Why?"

"Because I didn't do my homework."

"Oh. And now you do?"

Mark nodded.

"Well, maybe that's good. You really think he's too strict?"

"Of course *we* do," Paul said lightheartedly. "I mean we'd rather not do our homework, Dad. That's obvious, isn't it?" He laughed.

It was dark outside now. He put down *Call It Sleep* and got up off the bed and went from room to room on the second floor, pulling down shades and drawing curtains. In Stephanie's room, the messiest, he sat down on her bed for a moment. Amidst the bedside clutter, the paperback *Sunshine* caught his eye. Underneath the book, he picked up a notebook page covered with Stephanie's rather free-wheeling handwriting and began to read:

Things I Enjoy Most Out of Life

Warm fires inside on a cold day when it's raining or snowing or the wind is blowing. Taking long warm or hot baths in a dark room with the moonlight shining threw the windows. Sleeping. Awakening to a morning of dewy & crisp clear air & a fresh white sky. Listening to all different types of music. Dancing. Cool showers after a long hot bath or when I'm just hot. Exercising, laughing, reading, poetry, writing, playing with friends that I really like. Watching great old movies, eating, staying home from school, Christmas time! Giving, receiving, making people happy & making myself happy.

> Birthdays. Healthy foods, soft french bread, warm covers & a warm messy room. In summertime, visiting places like New York or the country, sachets, dresses, riding bikes...

"What!—are *you* doing?" Stephanie stood in the doorway of her room with her finger dramatically pointed at him, and smiling.

"I'm reading this great composition about things you like to do."

"Oh my God! You *know* you're not supposed to read my papers." She had rushed into the room and taken the page from him and was now combing the general bedside debris of books, magazines and papers for anything further of an off-limits variety.

"It wasn't personal, honey," he offered. "It was a very interesting paper. I found out you like warm messy rooms. No wonder we have a little problem here."

"Don't you *ever,* I mean *ever*..." Here she was hitting her dramatic-comic stride. Bette Davis to a nosy underling.

"I'm sorry," he said, smiling.

"Oh, it's okay," she said, abruptly dropping the act and sitting down on the blue and white rug among her things, sorting. "I don't really mind. But not without my permission, 'kay?"

"'Kay. How's school going?"

"Bad."

"Bad?"

"Well, not *bad* bad, but not good."

"What's the matter?"

"My social studies teacher hates me."

"I'm sure she doesn't *hate* you."

"She sure *acts* like she does."

"Like what?"

Paul made another gigantic thump downstairs. He would have to wrestle with him tonight. He would be leaving early the next morning and hopefully it would hold him for a couple of days. Boys were, after all, they had learned, different from girls, and their energy needed a force equal to their own to keep them from periodically wreaking havoc.

"Like calling on me when I was drawing instead of listening to her."

"Come on, Stephie. You're supposed to listen."

"I know. But I was just bored." She smiled at him rather sadly, the smile like a gesture of entreaty.

She loved to make intricate drawings of flowers, fairies and angels. She was also a natural writer—her school compositions could take off and far exceed the limits of the assignment, often to the teacher's understandable frustration, despite the evidence of a creative gift. An artist? It was not a course he could, in all honesty, recommend. But then that wasn't an issue. Artists didn't come about by recommendation. They did it because they couldn't do anything else. John Lennon said he would rather have been a fisherman.

They heard Paul ringing the dinner bell as if it was an Olympic event.

In bed with Betty past midnight, he massaged her shoulders and moved down her back and her waist and then held her firmly there. She liked it when he did this. She moved her leg over his leg. He kissed her back, now squeezing, now unsqueezing her waist.

She turned around and rested her head on his chest and held his shoulder, feeling his muscle. He moved his hand down her side and leaned down and found her lips. She kissed him and shied away after a moment.

She had a slow, sensuous body-time, and their foreplay could go on and on, with a number of intervals in which it might have been overtaken by sleep, but this was subterfuge on James's part, so that she would be less threatened by his tendency to move along.

At a certain point, he would turn over and kiss her, holding her, from above. This time her mouth would be warmer and, when things quickened, she would French kiss him for the first time in a darting way he loved.

Making love with Betty, it had occurred to him more than once, could be an earthly equivalent of heaven. It was sometimes as good as he could want, and he sometimes said things to this effect in the middle of their lovemaking. As the years had gone by and their lovemaking, sometimes after difficult, distant periods, had improved and deepened, he had recognized that it was the very heart of their marriage. If it could be good, with the world outside threatening in every conceivable posture, then they would be able to get through and go on.

In earlier years of their marriage, he would worry that some daytime rupture, humiliation or failure in his life or career might preempt his performance in bed, and sometimes this happened. But during these past several years, he had grown less anxious about the trials of his day life, and their love life had reached, in his sense of fundamental trust, greater heights—which they would then back away from somewhat. They seemed to be in one of these periods of retreat just now. For in each of them it was also a kind of self-dissolution and surrender, and especially for Betty, when balanced with her struggle to develop as an artist on top of her commitment as a mother, this could prove an exhaustion as well as a release. In the end, it was only as good as the feelings called up into their physical play, feelings that were inextricable from the physical play itself. Sometimes the moments would be filled with an almost absurd bounty. Then again, he could lose this contact and search for it for a week or two or longer with increasing restive doubt, wondering what he was doing and where he was going. Betty would turn over on her side after it was done and go to sleep without comment but he knew she was feeling deserted, alone and betrayed.

On the other hand, when they found themselves again, at the end, he would fall asleep with his mind echoing with all his worldly plans and efforts, while she held him, wrapped around him. He was quite naturally, it seemed, driven, picking up involuntarily just where he left off, while she was, in these minutes before sleep, less earthbound, and clung to him as if in some vertiginous realm of her own. If he wanted to destroy his own ceaseless and indestructible engine of identity through sex, her need seemed rather to bring her erotic life into closer rapport with her own worldly effort. It was the yin-yang of their years together, mixing and exchanging energy. She demanded a chase, but then, after the deed had been done, it was as if he found himself in a field with a fawn.

7

At the Los Angeles Airport Hertz office, he discovered he'd been booked into a silver Chevy Citation II. It was an overcast, intermittently sunny day. He had the radio on, and as he was driving down the Strip, in its daylight incarnation still somewhat sleepy-looking, he heard Prince's "Erotic City." In an electrified modification that made them seem the very voice of sexual hypnagogia, he and Sheila E. sang right over the LA airwaves about fucking all night long. Just beyond the Comedy Store, there was a young blond woman in silver hot pants with incredible white legs, walking.

When he checked into his twelfth floor room at the Beverly Hills Villa, he had two messages—one from Annette and one from Lazar Troy, an old New York friend, though how he knew he was in town, or where, was a mystery. James called Annette.

"Hi! You made it!" Her voice was, as always, revved and yet resonant of luxurious reserves, as though she had just eaten half a dozen butter cookies. "Listen, I've got a surprise!"

"What's that?" he answered a bit too levelly, sitting on the edge of his bed, looking out across Sunset Boulevard at the Beverly Hills flats. It was a white sky now with the sun making it yellow in one place.

"Hey, what is this? Sound happy! Sound thrilled! Sound like you're rich and famous and handsome and wonderful!"

"Gee," he said, standing up now and looking at the traffic on Sunset, "I just got off a plane, Annette, and anyway you know me too well for me to be very convincing on those counts."

"Of course I do, and you're adorable," she went on heedlessly. "But *listen*—we're doing UCLA."

"UCLA?"

"Yeah, there's some kind of film conference and they invited us both to be on the panel with Charles Champlin and your pal Oliver Hazen and a few others, I don't know who else."

It sounded interesting. At least Hazen did. He was a director around James's age whom he knew slightly and had admired for years. "When's this?"

"At three this afternoon!"

She gave him instructions to the auditorium, told him how excited she was he was here and that they were seeing Lindy Ramen tomorrow afternoon at Fox, and hung up. He put down the phone and stood before the low-set panorama of the Beverly Hills flats. Here were lives of every conceivable variety of power, sexuality, compromise, kinkiness, and wealth. He sat down on his bed again, as if made queasy by the vista alone.

He opened the drawer of his night table. Over the Gideon Bible lay a copy of the current issue of *Pent-*

house, which a former occupant had kindly left. He glanced at the flexed buttocks in the back shot of the cover girl, shut the drawer, and got up and went into the bathroom and ran a bath. He had a couple of hours before he met Annette and he needed to get unpacked and cleaned up for his public outing. As he was coming out of the bathroom, removing his shirt, the phone rang.

"Hello."

"Hello, hello, hello?" It was his friend's mock–Santa Claus voice. Beleaguered basso profundo.

"Hey, Lazar. How'd you know I was in town?"

"Your name's in the paper, man," he answered, his voice normal now, a slight New York tang to it. "You're at the UCLA Film Festival, right?"

"Yeah, that's what I hear."

"So I figured you'd be at the Villa. How 'bout dinner?"

His friend could be crazy but he sounded, at the moment, all right. "Sounds okay, but I'm gonna have to play it by ear with Annette Reed."

"All right, you're a busy man, big guy. How 'bout breakfast tomorrow at the Villa? They got a nice little place, you know."

They made the date, and he hung up and went to turn off the bath water. Then he unpacked his carry-on hanger-bag. He laid the copy of *Call It Sleep* on the night table. Whenever he came to LA, he made it a habit to bring along a good, demanding book, as ballast.

* * *

"I've never written a shot in my life," Oliver Hazen told his fellow panelists and the audience at the film festival. "The script is like a blueprint, the fundamental architecture of the film set down in scenes and dialogue. When you shoot it, then you discover the shots."

"Mr. Redding?" Charles Champlin turned graciously toward him, having caught his eye just a moment earlier.

"Well, since I'm a screenwriter who doesn't direct, one of the last of a dying breed, I'm told"—a little laugh rippled through the audience here; it was his Gore Vidal imitation—"I'm not qualified to comment on what Oliver has said, beyond saying that I admire his films very much, especially *American Dimes.* But I have an idea about film that I'd like to try out on the panel and the audience."

"Which is?" Champlin smiled.

The audience had packed the five-hundred-seat auditorium and there were people standing at the back as well. It was an old idea, the initial impetus behind certain scenes in *London Bridge,* but he'd never gone on record with it and now was his opportunity to make film history. He talked about chemistry in film being a product of reaction shots, sometimes entirely nonverbal. Someone in the audience called out for an example. By this time the idea seemed not only old, but shamelessly appropriated, stolen. If Betty had been there, she would have kicked him under the table.

"Well, I'd say—to use a nonpersonal example, because I think Annette did a lot of this in *London Bridge*—look at the dinner table scene in *My Brilliant Career,* where Jillian Armstrong intercuts between the fatuous suitor and Judy Davis and Sam Neil. Everything—humor, romance, character—happens with hardly a line spoken. It's a great scene in film language, which is I guess what Oliver is talking about, after all." He hoped it was a fairly graceful exit.

After the panel discussion was over, he said hello backstage to Hazen, a short, stocky man in his late thirties, who was looking better-rested than the last time James had seen him, one night at Area in Manhattan several months before. Hazen congratulated him on *London Bridge* and they chatted for a few moments. He felt a kind of easy familiarity with Hazen that required no particular effort.

"What're you doing tonight?" the director asked him.

"Nothing, as far as I know. I have to check with Annette."

"We're having dinner together. Do you want to join us?"

"Sure, if I won't be in the way."

"She's about to ask you herself."

In the evening gray, just before the darkness settled in, he followed Annette and Hazen in her cream Rolls, with a vanity license that read DIRECTOR, to Ma Maison. By the time he got there it was night. He got out of his Citation and the valet parking attendant, who looked like a lifeguard misplaced in the subaqueous precinct of the nighttime parking lot, recognized him.

"Hi, Mr. Redding. Good to see you again."

"Thank you."

He entered the restaurant and was led to the table where Annette and Oliver were already seated. A few booths away John Dunne and Joan Didion sat, quietly engrossed in conversation with each other.

"One of our royal couples," he said, sitting down at the table and smiling toward the Dunnes' table.

"Oh, please," Annette said. "I'm so bored with their chic. They've cultivated it so tirelessly. They're two of the shrewdest team players in the business and they'd just as soon cut your throat as look at you."

"Well!" James answered, as a sort of conversational ventilator. Hazen laughed.

"Anyway," James added, "it's the Reagan era."

"What's that supposed to mean?" Annette looked at him with her dead-on, depthless and very dark eyes. She was wearing a black sweater that further demonized her dark features. Suddenly he realized he didn't have the slightest clue about her politics.

"I know what he means," Hazen interjected politely. Like Annette, he was a veteran Hollywood hardball player, but his career had been controversial and full of ambiguities, like his decision to relocate in New York a few years earlier.

"I feel I'm at the hub of an enigma," James interjected in his best effort at a magisterial voice with an English accent.

Hazen laughed; Annette continued to eyeball him.

"You just be perfect tomorrow," she told him, vis-à-vis nothing he had said. Perhaps she sensed some wayward instinct in him she would need to squelch in Lindy's presence?

"Well, you tell me," he said to Annette. She was, after all, at this point, his boss.

"Tell you what?" she said, her head now in her menu.

"I mean how do you want me to behave at the meeting?"

"Nothing special, kid. This is social for you, business for me. Think of yourself as pillow stuffing." She had lowered her menu and now smiled ghoulishly at him.

"Oh, thanks. I'm a human bolster pillow? Tell me this. Whose ass is it gonna be in my face?" What? He had done it again—lost it, right out here in public.

By degrees Annette's look hardened until it was metallic, mythic, terrible. "You mind your language, mister, or you find yourself someone else to do your bidding."

In his mind there was a swirling chaos. They were going to take away the Miró drawing, and the Dufy etching of heaven, the Early American pine chest of drawers, and the silver, and the gold. Orthodontia would no longer be discussable for his children. A For Sale sign would be posted on his lawn, a yard sale in his driveway with his brand-new chainsaw going for peanuts. Betty would look at him in a certain way, her life a mistake because she had gotten it involved with his life. His children would see the naked face of failure. It would be his face.

"Annette," he answered, looking at her with newfound urgency and sincerity, "please accept my apology. I'm joking. You said pillow stuffing—I self-protectively made a joke, that's all. I mean I do have *some* ego, and I think I need it."

She continued to look at him, as if coolly searching his face for an article of faith, or the absence of it, and then, abruptly, she nodded and muttered something about ordering. Hazen signaled a waiter, who came to the table to take their orders. He had pulled an apology out of himself a lot better than the old waiter at the Russian Tea Room. But then, he was a younger man, working for more money.

They enjoyed their wine, dinner, dessert and coffee, and more or less desultory conversation.

"But there is a kind of tightness in the air now," he ventured boldly, feeling almost himself again in the euphoria of the end of the meal, tempting fate. By this time, however, he was fairly certain Hazen had similar feelings.

"It's like a certain kind of leader," the director said, looking at him "say a Gandhi or a Martin Luther King, breathes pure oxygen into his constituency, his country, and even into history. Whereas with another kind of leader, no matter what the economy may be, or all the other variables—and a lot of them are godawful right now—it's as if something is gone, some vital element is at a famine level."

"Yeah, that's it," James said, as if feeling a charge of oxygen himself. "I mean here I am; for the first time in my life, I'm doing well, and my wife and kids are well taken care of, and I'm..."

"You're guilty as hell, and you're scared shitless someone's gonna take it away from you and you may even be ready to fuck up just to avoid all that suspense and fear."

"What I like about you, Annette," James said, smiling, "is the sense I have of your solid-as-a-rock, abiding confidence in me."

She didn't bat an eyelash; or even slightly smile.

"You don't *need* my confidence," she told him. "In the first place, you've got all the arrogance you'll ever need, and in the second place, the key to your talent—which, I think you know, I have the greatest respect for; or what have I been doing for three years?—is your ability to absorb and handle challenges, including reversals, including maybe even humiliations. You *need* that kind of anxiety, James, because you're much, much too complacent otherwise."

"You sound like my father," he said seriously.

"Well," she answered, now smiling, "I know how much you loved *him,* so I'm taking that as a compliment. Listen," she said, now turning to Hazen, "don't keep him up too late tonight. I want him fresh for Lindy tomorrow; although since it's not till three, you'll have a little leeway. I'm going home." She stood up now, and he and Hazen stood as well.

"Good night, Annette," James said. "See you tomorrow."

"Good night," she said, as he and Hazen both kissed her good-bye.

Albert's, a club on the corner of Franklin and Highland, had a trio made up of piano, bass and drums, and sitting at a table in a darkened corner of the room with Hazen two hours later, James realized how much he loved hearing an acoustic bass solo: it was like hearing music in shadow. The effort of articulation, the melody trying to escape the limits of a percussion instrument, had such a powerfully resonant presence. The bassist was black, very tall and thin. Leaning over the bass, he worked it hard with long, nimble fingers. When the piano and drums came back in again on Miles Davis's "Nardis," he felt an interior surge.

"What about *your* father?" he asked Hazen, both of them now pleasantly high.

"My dad was a failure," Hazen said matter-of-factly. "Used to direct plays at the Pasadena Playhouse, taught acting classes, would take character parts in TV series now and then. *I* thought he was a failure, and I hated the whole show-business shtick."

"You never talked with him?" James asked, and sipped his beer.

"Not for a long, long time. I was this hotshot intellectual at USC, writing about Kurosawa and the French New Wave, and then reviewing movies for the LA *Free Press.* I was married, and I was real serious, and I was bored, and I was unhappy. And then my wife left me." Hazen smiled here. "She went off with this goddamn fisherman who wanted to live in Australia. And I kind of hit bottom."

"Geez," James said and didn't smile.

"Yeah. So my dad's just gotten this mortgage on this summer theater down in Orange County. Actually it's just a broken-down barn he wants to *make into* a summer theater again. By this time he's in his sixties, two broken marriages behind him, and now I'm at loose ends, and he calls me up and says, 'I hear your wife left you.' So I said, 'Yeah, she did,' and he says, 'Come down and help your old broken-down father put this summer theater together, would you please?'"

"He sounds funny."

"Funny? In a way, I guess. Show-business funny. He probably got all those lines out of some play. But he knew something about me—more than I thought he knew. So I go down there and he and I and this Italian kid named Joe Santini, who's now a TV director, built this theater. I mean we made the stage, created the lighting system, rigged up the curtain pulleys. And all this time, like two months, April and May of 1970, we just work and eat and sleep. And my Dad doesn't ask me about Donna, my wife, in fact we don't really talk at all, but I notice I'm beginning to come back, you know?"

"Getting strong again." James caught the eye of a brunette in a party of people at the next table, who smiled and he smiled back and then looked back at Hazen. Good-looking women were everywhere.

"Getting strong again," Hazen said, looking at him with a small smile. "Anyway, then the summer season starts and I build sets and work as a stage manager and then my father asks me to do the male lead in this old romantic comedy workhorse, *Boys and Girls Together*. I'd done a few things with him before but I wasn't really into acting. So—I have this big scene with the female lead, and he's got me clear across the stage from her. I say to him, 'Pop, this is a love scene. I gotta be closer to her.' And he gets really heavy about it: 'You stay where you are. Don't move!' He kept us like that until the night before we opened and then he closed the gap. But he tells me, 'Play it *exactly* the same as you've been playing it.' And it turned out he was right, because he kept me so far away from her that I had to put everything into the emotion: I had no 'business' I could fake it with, I couldn't *do* anything. And it made me give a good performance... The son of a bitch was a director."

"Like father like son, hunh?"

"There he was: broke and in his sixties, and a little over two years later, he had a heart attack and died. But he put Humpty Dumpty back together again."

It occurred to James that he and Hazen were both on official business trips—here today, gone the next—which sometimes, he had noticed, precipitated an intimacy that would have been unlikely within the precincts of their daily routines. American men seemed to tell their deepest stories to one another on airplanes, or during stopovers in terminal restaurants, at the tail end of official long-distance calls, or during similar interims in which the time element pressurized the narrative, and at the same time promised an immediate release from intimacy.

"That's a beautiful story, Oliver."

"Think it would make a movie?" Hazen winked at him.

His bed had been turned down for him in his room at the Villa, and the curtains closed but for a few feet that showed the Beverly Hills streets, now twinkling in the night. He stood for a moment in front of this vista, then closed the curtains all the way, and switched the TV on. There was a late news segment, showing Daniel Ortega jogging in Central Park. Here was this man, perhaps younger than he was, the head of a nation in an undeclared war with America, showing up in New York and jogging with his bodyguards in Central Park. The newscaster reported that Ortega was in New York to address the United Nations General

Assembly as part of the UN's fortieth anniversary ceremony. He also said that a state of emergency had been declared in Nicaragua and the newspaper *La Prensa* had been censored. What was going on? Ortega looked strong and somewhat stolid. He had spent years in prison under the Somoza regime. It was smart of him to go on American television to let everyone see a human face behind the headlines, playing Reagan's game back at him.

He undressed and got into bed with the television still on with the sound turned down, and picked up *Call It Sleep.* His mind was racing ahead or lagging behind the speed of the sentences, and he had to read the page over a second time. This time he broke through to the extraordinary clarity of the story, its stately rhythms delineating a lost world: the turn-of-the-century Jewish immigrant community on the Lower East Side. The mother's memories of Eastern European culture, the father's torment in the New World. On an impulse, he pressed the book to his face and breathed in its musty fragrance. Looking back at the television, he saw that there was now pornography on the screen. He put the book down on the night table.

It seemed to have been filmed in Europe and featured a beautiful, leggy blond wearing a minidress and no underwear while riding a Moped around the streets of the city, which looked like Rome, and unnerving everyone with the view she so blithely put forward. She even pulled up at a gas station, and the attendant filled her tank, going cross-eyed in the process. It was rather good-natured, tongue-in-cheek pornography, obviously European as opposed to the strictly meat-and-potatoes American variety. It was also ridiculous. He finally switched off the TV and then the bed-table lamp and lay in the room's sudden darkness, trying to feel its parameters. He was still hopelessly wide awake. After a moment, he turned on the light again, remembering the copy of *Penthouse* in the night-table drawer.

After looking through the photo spreads, he turned to the "Forum" section, where readers wrote in about their sexual adventures. In one letter, a successful professional woman wrote that she is often on the road and has had very good luck at picking up attractive women. Possessed of a strikingly good figure that she keeps in shape with exercise, at a recent convention in a Midwestern city she struck up a conversation with a smashing redhead with exquisite pale skin, who told her she was attending the convention without her husband. In a friendly, casual manner the correspondent asked the redhead if she would like to join her that evening at her hotel for a jog and then dinner. The woman accepted. That evening in the hotel room as they both began to change into their running costumes, the writer, who had removed her top, noticed that the redhead was staring, apparently mesmerized, at her breasts, which she wrote were very full and, because of her exercise regimen, didn't sag. Sensing that things were heating up faster than she had anticipated, she asked the redhead to assist her in putting on her running bra and tossed it over to her. The redhead was visibly trembling as she helped. Then, suddenly stuttering, she asked the correspondent how she kept breasts as big as hers from sagging.

As if opting for a breath of air, James broke off his reading here and looked up for a moment into the stillness of his hotel room. There was some sort of motorized hum on the air, the usual hotel room's midnight drone, and the faraway honk of a car somewhere below. Were these the secret stories of real-life America? Or had they all been made up by the readers and/or the editors of the magazine? After a moment, he went back to the hot-house narrative.

The woman told her guest that she would show her some exercises for her bosom. She then suggested that she help the redhead into her outfit. The woman undressed and her breasts proved to be as big as the writer's with very big aureoles and nipples the size of thimbles. And they were almost as firm as the correspondent's. As she assisted the redhead, the bra rubbed one of the woman's apparently very sensitive aureoles too roughly and she let out a little cry of pain. The correspondent wrote that she apologized profusely and, sensing an opening here, began to gently stroke the area. Almost at once, evidently losing control of herself, her guest began to strain her breast upward into the woman's touch. The writer continued her stroking and slowly leaned down and kissed the chafed breast, and now the woman let out a sigh. They didn't go for the run. In a little while the writer was licking, nibbling, and sucking both of the redhead's urgent breasts. Later on, her guest, apparently unable to any longer fight off her desire, was licking, slurping and sucking the businesswoman's pussy. The woman wrote that she was tremendously turned on to have a woman with a husband doing what the redhead did for her.

She said that over the course of the week they were at the convention together, the truly unexpected happened: she fell in love with the redhead.

He read episode after episode, by turns riveted, aroused, and appalled, until he felt like he was drowning in a sea of semen, pussy fluids, and sweat. All of the narratives had a strangely elusive but persistent undercurrent: they all somehow had to do with power. The most obvious manifestation was the size of everyone's parts: big, bigger, and biggest. And the moment of truth somehow had to do with the primacy of one's needs over another's. The lady executive is gratified by the fact that a woman with a husband would do what the redhead does for her. She has a woman gratifying *her* instead of her husband and this is what moves her most. It was late-capitalist merger-mania sex, corporeal—as opposed to corporate—takeovers. The letters went on and on, and James's brain and body grew, respectively, delirious and exhausted. Finally, he put the magazine back in the drawer and turned off the light again.

8

He sat bolt upright in bed, opened his eyes and discovered his hotel room in the half-lit, undersea coziness of morning before the curtains admitted the day. Had he just gasped for air as his daughter had done a couple of nights ago? There wasn't anybody to tell him. He sat for a moment, breathing regularly, and then lay back on his pillow. He turned to the clock radio on the night table. It was five past seven. He had forgotten to phone for a wake-up call the night before. He would have to get up. His breakfast with Lazar was for nine, and he had a few things he wanted to do in the meantime: exercise, phone Betty, make some notes for the meeting with Lindy Ramen.

It dawned on him that he had woken from a nightmare. He had been given a head transplant: his new hair in the dream was black and thickly curly, his face pallorous and thick-featured. Somehow he needed to ingratiate himself with an old whore whose body had gone and whose teeth were loose in their sockets. He tried to explain himself to her and then met her mouth in a kiss. Though he needed to maintain the impression of casual affection, he immediately wondered whether he had infected himself with AIDS.

A *head* transplant? Well, here he was in the heart of Babylon Revisited, obviously a potent resource for his dream life: he'd untangle it some other time. Today might be the day they gave him more money. They might send him a check soon that would impress the youthful, rotund officer at his local bank. He would be looked upon as an important customer even if he arrived on the premises unshaven and wearing his jeans jacket. And what had he done for it all? It wasn't *The Zoo Story,* it wasn't *Howl,* and it wasn't *Look Back in Anger*. But maybe it had a little charm (a bit of *Billy Liar,* maybe?). It was a script about a guy like himself, on the loose after hitting it big with a best-selling novel. Every attractive woman he looks at induces an instantaneous fantasy. Frequently he sees them naked (enter eager studio executives).

He got up out of bed and went into the shower. The miracle of life began to repossess his mind and body under the hotel's powerful water pressure. In the move from horizontal to vertical he began to reclaim a rough approximation of his identity.

After drying off and shaving, he put on a pair of black drawstring short pants. He drew open the curtains on another warmish, dull white day, and went through the aerobics in his exercise book for day five in a seven-day series. Now winded, he switched on the television, keeping the sound off, and went over to the phone, sitting down on his bed to call Betty.

He got his own voice on his answering machine. "Hi, Betty," he told the machine and left her a brief message and said he would phone back later. It wasn't yet eleven there and, with the kids off to school, maybe she had gone to work in her studio and disconnected her extension.

He finished dressing and sat down at the writing table beside the television to write his notes for the afternoon meeting. He needed a one-line summary of the whole movie: something Lindy Ramen could pass on to other executives at Fox like a skeleton key to all the doors of the budget. It's the story of a man who gets everything he ever wanted—and it's too much. It's the story of a man who gets everything he ever wanted—and he nearly dies in a butterfat coma. He needed Annette there. Someone to sting his mind into a respectful sobriety.

Lazar Troy, thin, dark, saturnine, was downstairs at the Pink Teacup in a corner booth at the back when James arrived at nine. He waved to him and made his way back. He sat down and the elderly waitress poured coffee for him before he had gotten all the way into his seat.

"Mr. LA casual, huh?" Lazar said, surveying him with broad skepticism.

James had decided on a blue open-collar shirt with a navy blue sweater over his shoulders, jeans, and white Nikes. LA was a physical town, a body-count town. The idea was Be There—With Your Body. "You don't like the threads?" he countered.

"Hey," Lazar told him jovially, sitting in his own darker, more brooding costume of blazer over black shirt, jeans, and James couldn't see what shoes, "you look like the greatest fuckin' writer since Pat Boone."

"Okay, Mr. Nice Guy," James answered and made as if to get up and leave.

Lazar laughed, pulled him back, and said in a more friendly, perhaps even a pleading voice, "Sorry. We're sorry. Very sorry. You know we love you, ducks."

"Get with it, Lazar," he told him, smiling. "Or I'm gonna haf to power-pound you."

"Yo, Rocky!" his friend came back. "Seriously, man, I'm happy to see you and I'm happy you're such a big success and everything. And, oh, I knew there was something I wanted to tell you. Guess who showed up at my house last night with his new wife and *two* tiny little babies?"

"Who?" James said, putting his coffee back down, suddenly hungry.

"Elvin Fleischer."

"Elvin?" He was an old New York friend, a playwright who had had a small success years ago for a verse play based on *The Odyssey.*

"Yep. Without his trenchcoat—but lookin' okay, you know. I don't know if I ever quite said it to you but I used to think he was like a close second to Shakespeare, I worshiped the guy. Then he ran off with..." As if distracted suddenly, Lazar signaled the little waitress with her blond beehive, a woman who must have been close to seventy. He had an elegant way with a gesture of this kind. He moved and carried himself a little like Sinatra.

"Ellen?" James helped him along.

"Yeah, Ellen. In fact when he ran off with Ellen, I

wanted to kill him, her, myself. A multiple-choice question, check all three." He started laughing.

"What'll it be, boys?" the waitress said at their side. She was a cute lady, a grandmotherly waitress, just the right touch at the Villa where the lines of coke got snorted off the lines of contracts with trick clauses.

"Eggs Benedict. And when you get a chance more coffee, sweetheart," Lazar said.

"Same for me," James said to her.

"Comin' up, fellas."

"Right out of *Seven Brides for Seven Brothers,* isn't she?" Lazar said fondly as she went off.

"No kidding. This is some bunkhouse. So what's with Elvin right now?"

"What's he up to? Right at the moment, he's at my house. His wife is at their home somewhere in East LA. I can't make him out exactly. He wanted to come and see you but I said I'd bring you back if you have time. I think he's going to put the touch on me, and you too, if you decide to come back, but I figured I'd give you a choice."

"I'd like to see him."

At the entrance of the Villa, after breakfast, they got into Lazar's red Porsche—Lazar tipping the parking attendant—and drove into the Hollywood hills. Lazar's new apartment seemed to have been stuck onto the side of a rock and its value had more to do with the view, a sweeping one of all the houses and pools below, than with anything afforded by the shallow, half-empty two rooms and the narrow fringe of balcony.

Elvin Fleischer was at first invisible in the strange cross-traffic of indoor and outdoor light in the apartment, but then James saw him standing by the refrigerator in the tiny kitchenette and beaming at him, blond, stocky, not noticeably older looking, and dressed in a white leisure shirt over white chinos, like a tourist at his beloved Acropolis somehow transplanted to West Hollywood.

"Elvin."

"Jamie."

They embraced. It was a hug, James supposed, that said time by itself was a miracle and even if they had never gotten along that well, they had shared this profound element.

After the obligatory tour of the apartment, or the apartment's view—poor Lazar needed a woman's touch; he hadn't a clue how to live—the three settled around the glass-topped living-room table, James with a cup of instant decaf, Lazar and Elvin with a joint. The next thing he knew, the mood was all haywire. He should have remembered Lazar was a moody guy.

"I'm getting married again, man," he told James out of the blue with a look and tone that somehow seemed to contain a threat.

"Wonderful," he said, switching into his Mr. Lucky persona, his social utility infielder, all around the town. He had known Lazar's first wife, a pretty Italian girl named Brenda, and his friend's bitterness after their breakup.

"Yeah," Lazar said, as if momentarily eased by James's casual reply, "wanna see a picture of her?"

"Sure."

He took out his wallet and passed along a small close-in color snapshot, showing a pretty young woman in daylight with a pronounced cleavage. James passed it along to Elvin who, hunched over on his seat, pondered it for what seemed a very long time.

James was aware that he was picking up a contact high and was proud of himself for abstaining. Marijuana had been his drug of choice and it had taken Betty to get him to clean up his act. It made him into a sloppy, delighted fool.

"Got any other photographs?" Elvin asked, suddenly looking up.

"You bet," Lazar snapped back. From the top of his refrigerator, he passed them a polaroid of an erect cock about to receive a blow job from a different woman than appeared in the first photograph. The photograph had been taken by the man about to receive the blow job.

"Is this...you?" Elvin asked as he held the photograph forward, now sitting up in his chair, so that both he and James could see it.

"Uh-huh."

James took the photograph from Elvin, studied it for a moment, and then put it down on the table.

"Well," he said, "gotta go."

Elvin started laughing, James followed, and finally Lazar joined in. They laughed for a while. A little later Elvin told James he was translating the *Aeneid,* working from a French text. It was an original concept that had gained the praise of poets and scholars. Later on, Lazar, who had recently started his own production company after years as a film editor, stood up and said vehemently to them both: "I *own* Warren Beatty." This was extreme even in Lazar's megalomaniacal mood, and James realized the grass must have been sinsemilla, and that he really needed to get out into the day.

"Not working today?" he asked Lazar.

"I phone in," Lazar answered and shrugged.

James called for a taxi and was driven back to the Villa. Elvin hadn't put the touch on him. Perhaps he'd forgotten in his marijuana haze and would catch hell from his wife when he went home. His room was immaculate again, the day outside now a white glare. He sat down on his bed and began to dial Betty's number but was interrupted by a knock on the door. It was twelve twenty. He got up and went over to the door and opened it. A pretty, freckled mulatto woman, quite tall, wearing the hotel's staff apron, smiled at him and asked sleepily, "Service?"

"Service?" he answered, confused.

"Yes," she said, her smile not hurrying, not departing. She really was pretty, also nicely built, her breasts in a maroon T-shirt evident on each side of the navy blue apron. He immediately imagined her naked—and himself, fucking her. Her presence introduced a kind of involuntary narcolepsy into his being. He suddenly felt half-dead with excitement.

"Well, I'm not sure—is the room already finished?"

"No—dusting," she said and moved past him at the door with authority. He caught a whiff of some perfume: Jungle Gardenia, maybe?

At his bed table—the door gone *bam!* shut behind

them—she began dusting with a yellow cloth in a somewhat half-assed manner.

In another instant he noticed he was growing thick with the excitement of this incomprehensible intruder.

"Oh," she said, for she had now opened the bed-table drawer, "*Penthouse!* Naughty boy! But you wanna know something?"

"Sure," he said. Nothing like a hard-on to make him feel secure, engrossed, happy with the world.

Now she was sitting on his bed, turned around to face him with the magazine opened in front of her. "Those girls are so overendowed. I mean you wanna fuck a truck?"

"I know what you mean," he said, grinning sheepishly, still standing in the middle of the room.

"I'm right, aren't I?" She was from somewhere else, but just where he'd have trouble guessing. Mexico? Iran? Las Vegas, maybe? The day outside had shrunk to irrelevancy—fuck 'em all.

"I'm better. Promise not to tell?"

"Promise," he said, deep in ecstatic idiocy. His cock was pointing through his jeans to the window. Nothing like this had ever happened to him and he was ready to kiss the earth in gratitude.

"You're not making fun of me, are you?" On the contrary, he knew she was, in her way, much smarter than he was. She was even smarter, in her way, than Reva Makepeace, Annette Reed, maybe even Lindy Ramen (well, that one was a conundrum to put on hold, a Zen koan to examine carefully later, but not to worry just now).

"No," he said loudly. "Not at all." He didn't care now if she saw his hard-on or not.

Suddenly the apron was down and she pulled the T-shirt up over her head. She was rather delicately put together, with thin freckled shoulders, poignant shoulders. Her breasts were also freckled with asymmetrical strawberry-colored aureoles. They were special breasts, personal ones.

She held one breast in one hand without looking at it, but at him. "It's true, isn't it? Better than *that*..."—indicating the magazine with her free hand. It lay open to an artistic study of a blonde, her breasts patterned with sunlight spilt through bamboo slats.

"Yes, better," he said.

His heart was in his throat; his pulse was in his neck. She took his hand and said, "Sit down."

He sat down and she unzipped him and took out his hard-on and sucked it. Then, after he undressed and put on a condom he got out of the small zippered compartment of his carry-on bag, he fucked her. She operated her pussy with muscular expertise, but he went at her with surprising hunger for quite a long and intense time, occasionally licking or sucking one of her breasts, which she accommodatingly proffered from beneath him on the bed. He had never felt so hard in his life; while she felt lithe and lemony. When he came, he felt a compounding of so many corners of his being, he could have disappeared.

"Oh," she said, as they both were breathing heavily at the end while he kept it in her to the hilt, "nice."

Afterward, they took a shower together, and he gave her a hundred dollars from his wallet. Her name was Anita, she told him. She was from Camarillo. She gave him a piece of paper with her first name and a phone number with an 805 area code written on it. Then, after getting dressed and reassuming the apron, she left.

"See you," she said at the door.

"Thank you," he answered mindlessly, relaxed.

The Villa was known as a haven for some of the most famous rock 'n' rollers and perhaps its services had a larger variety than he had, in several previous stays there, suspected. Or maybe it was just people hustling in the halls in costumes they'd acquired to stay clear of the management. He had crossed the line.

Betty was still out.

After phoning ahead for clearance, they let him drive through the Fox gate. He found a parking spot and was directed to Lindy Ramen's office on the fifth floor. He was two or three minutes early. After declining coffee from the smiling, middle-aged female receptionist, he sat down on the broad, dark green sofa with a low wood table running the length of it. There was a copy of *Variety* and one of *People* on the table but he didn't pick either one of them up. Then Annette came in, wearing a white blouse and a dark suit, looking very fresh and stoked up.

"Hello, kid," she said softly yet urgently as he stood up to kiss her. "You look smashing."

"So do you."

"Is she here?" she asked in a bigger voice.

"She's got someone in with her, Annette," the receptionist told her, "but she should be finished any minute. Would you like some coffee or anything?"

"Nothing for me, sweetie," Annette said to her. "How 'bout you, James?"

He shook his head no and they sat down on the sofa together. He picked up the copy of *People* with the Achille Lauro story on the cover and skimmed it for a few minutes.

Suddenly the door to Lindy's office opened, and a harried-looking young man in his shirt-sleeves emerged, nodded to the receptionist, and walked out determinedly. Lindy, in a dark flower-print dress, appeared in her doorway, and waved them both into her office.

He and Annette stood up and walked in, and Lindy closed the door behind them. Annette and Lindy hugged, and then he shook Lindy's hand.

"Hi, James," she said easily. "Good to see you."

"Good to see *you,* Lindy."

She was in her mid-twenties, mid-*twenties,* of medium height, wore little or no makeup, and had a great deal of long brown hair. She had a small, rather long face with large, attractive eyes. There was also the famous bosom, rather too big for his taste and somewhat mobile behind the busy green and blue pattern of her sheath dress.

James and Annette took seats on the small black sofa and Lindy pulled up a chair.

"Have you had a chance to read the script, baby doll?" Annette asked her keenly.

"Of course I've read it," she beamed back at the director.

"Isn't it—like candy?" Annette said and glanced proudly over at James.

"Like candy," Lindy seconded. "But you know what I kept wondering, Annette and James?"

Here it comes, he thought. He remembered her telling him that *London Bridge* was based on character and their computer had told them that that was a negative in today's market, dismissing the entire Western humanist tradition with one printout. Here he was, then, in a room with two female captains of industry: Annette, a diminutive genius in her mid-thirties, who got her way with a brash directness except perhaps in the presence of the other, an even younger woman who was rumored to have arrived at her current eminence via an affair with Al Abbott, the man in charge of the whole company. What had Lindy done for Abbott in exchange for this particular favor? James could see potential here. But his mind must not be allowed to mutiny right at the moment of truth. He was, it occurred to him, an almost irrelevant touch in this high-powered chamber, really no more than decorative—like a gun moll.

"I kept wondering who we could get to do him," Lindy told them both, smiling.

Not so bad as last time.

"Lindy, Lindy, Lindy..." Annette stood up now and walked around to the back of Lindy's chair and put her hands on Lindy's shoulders and Lindy raised her arms and took Annette's hands in her own hands. "Will you look at this girl, James?" she said, looking at him on the sofa. "Will you look at this *woman?* Alright, she's beautiful." Lindy flushed slightly and looked away from James. Perhaps he would one day fuck her, after all.

He kept the look of warm, loving appreciation that had flooded his features, as though he were witnessing something delightful yet at the same time very moving. But caught up as he was in this female hot-house of a bargaining table, he was having difficulty keeping his errant mind in check. What if he suddenly, involuntarily, asked Lindy what an attractive young woman like her saw in an old beer barrel like Al Abbott? She would most likely flush and then harden and he would be put out of the office, his career ruined, and Annette would perhaps personally come to his house and have him beaten while she stood watching. It would be the moral equivalent of yelling "Fuck!" during an interview with Jane Pauley on *Today*. (Perhaps an idea for *Success!—?*)

"Please, Annette. Stop it," Lindy said, looking up at her now, smiling.

"Wait, Lindy. Because that's only one side of the story. Because do you know what this woman really is, James, after you get past all of that? She's the single shrewdest and most knowing studio executive in the business today. She's got the American heartbeat in her little pinky. And you want to know *why* that is?" He nodded, beaming. "Because she's never forgotten where she comes from..."

The San Fernando Valley?

"Sherry maybe forgot her roots," Annette continued, "but not Lindy. Lindy's too smart to forget."

She let go of Lindy's hands now and walked from the back of her chair a few feet over to a position from which she could look at both of them. He knew he was witnessing one of Annette's A meetings. Why then did he feel like an aquarium from which all water had been drained, a forgotten appurtenance, once colorful and alive, now empty and scum-stained. His ego was at ground zero, and the trick, he knew, was not to say anything, to remain mute, mum, dumb—until the final amenities. It was simple. American business was going about its daily routine—he was on a veritable magic-carpet ride. Let the girls call the shots; he'd be well taken care of. His ability to write was as great a gift as beauty had been in a woman of his mother's generation.

From his seat, he looked back and forth at the two of them and then he caught Lindy's eye, smiling at him as if to say, "Isn't this lady Annette the greatest thing since WD-40?" and he had a feeling they were getting along toward home free. As if on cue then, he had a terrifying impulse to erupt in a rebel yell of "Fuck! Shit! Cunt!" In an instantaneous cold sweat, he fought this impulse with everything he had. Breathe deeply, he told himself. Breathe deeply and notice your breathing.

9

Tuesday evening, walking through Kennedy Airport with his carry-on bag, he decided to give Joan Wallin a call. He was elated. Annette had kissed him warmly good-bye in the 20th Century–Fox parking lot after their meeting with Lindy. "You were adorable," she purred in his ear. They had spent about half an hour talking about details of the budget and Lindy was now going to have a detailed "under-the-line" worked up. That meant they were closer to a deal. At the same time, logistics had gotten fouled up with Betty. He'd finally caught her at home early that morning before he checked out of the Beverly Hills Villa. She told him she had a meeting with Tony Sears, the owner of her New York gallery, and would have to talk timetables later. Fine. He was back in New York and there was a little slack in the line. He figured it was now or never.

He took a seat in a row of open chrome telephone booths, and pressed the numbers under her name on the notepad page with the Carlyle letterhead. Her handwriting was small and even, listing just slightly rightward. She was a person who dotted her *is* with little circles. The phone rang twice, and she answered "Hello" with a voice that was pitched low and without a discernible coloration: a don't-start-anything-dumb voice.

"Hello, is this Joan Wallin?"

"Yes?"

A tall blond woman in toreador pants wheeled a collapsible stroller by his booth. Abstractedly, he studied her moves. "Hi, this is James Redding. I spoke with you last Friday..."

Suddenly he was gasping for air and had to cover the mouthpiece of the phone lest she detect his spasm. During the first year of his work with Annette on the script of *London Bridge,* she had brought in a young woman named Marsha Stevenson, well-known in Hollywood as a script doctor, to punch up a number of scenes. They had met in their bathing suits at Annette's Bel Air poolside, and, on the second afternoon at this site, flushed with his newfound success but already feeling too much in thrall to Annette and her power axis, he had asked Stevenson what she was doing that night for dinner. So, it came to him now, during this interval of several seconds of silence to allow him to irrigate his throat, he had in fact tried this once before. Marsha Stevenson was an otherwise fairly ordinary-looking brunette who happened to have two legs that could kill: legs he had quickly found himself making the center of his imaginary world. She had looked back wryly at him after his invitation and asked him how old he was. When he answered thirty-seven, she made a whooplike noise, rested on her back on her towel again, and, looking straight up at the sky, told him: "Take a dime from my bag and call me when you're twenty."

A yuppie bitch.

"Oh, hi. Yes, I remember." The voice had changed, was warm and open. Shazam! James Redding and his magic name, movie, whatever it might be. It was reassuring, reassuring enough for him to recapture his speaking voice. Here was someone who liked him on the basis of the charade he'd just enacted in Hollywood, a sort of perk, as it were, of his newfound livelihood. Perhaps he even *deserved* her.

"Hi. I'm at Kennedy Airport; I just got in from LA. Anyway, if you have some time tonight, I'd love to buy you a drink and talk a little—for the article, I mean."

"I'd love to, but I'm sort of in my home clothes, and sort of looking forward to complete crowd control here. Would you mind stopping by and we could have the drink here?"

"That would be fine." He didn't want to put too strong a line under it. What was happening? Or could the lady simply be wonderfully relaxed and good-natured?

"Good. I've got some wine here, if that's okay. Otherwise, I'm afraid you'll have to pick up something."

"No problem," he answered, immediately regretting this TV teenager's phrase. "Where are you?"

"The address here is 53 West Eighty-first Street, and I'm number fourteen-A."

So much for the walk-up. The veils were rising. "Okay, I'll probably pick up some beer and see you around, oh, say eight-thirty or nine?"

"Great," she said amiably. "That makes it a lot easier for me."

For me too, he uttered only in the darkening comedy of his mind. "See you then," he added out loud to Joan Wallin.

He came to a red light at the corner of Broadway and Ninety-sixth. Funk city. Everybody with their own personal stride inscribing the neon-lit scene. Quite loud, too, under his radio. Whitney Houston bringing the soul of the middle-aged American man to attention.

He found a parking spot on Columbus near Eighty-third Street, parked, locked up, and went into a deli on the corner. He got a six-pack of Miller Lite and, at the last minute, went to the stationery shelf and picked out a small blue spiral notepad. The reporter persona might come in handy. He should probably make the article about bookstores just to maintain strictest sincerity.

The night outside was chillier than he'd realized. He was wearing a blazer over a workshirt, along with jeans and an expensive pair of Italian shoes that now, after two years, were finally softening into a reasonably comfortable fit. He passed the windows of the Endicott bookstore without even a cursory stop.

He walked west on Eighty-first Street, found the number, and entered the building. In the big, over-lit front lobby, he found the 14A buzzer and pressed it. "Yes?" came her voice, stripped of all modulation. "Hi, it's James Redding." The buzzer rang; he moved to the door and was clicked through. He rode up to fourteen (the next floor after 12), taking a few shots of a health-food-store breath freshener he'd discovered in his pocket, and the door sprang open. Too quickly. He got out onto a small, sepia-carpeted corridor. Fourteen-A was the door on the right at one end of the hall. He rang the bell and in a moment she opened the door.

"Hi," she said, smiling, he thought, just a little wryly. She was wearing a men's white shirt that she let hang over her blue jeans, and she was barefoot. Her hair was pinned up all piecemeal with bobby pins and miscellaneous strands around her ears and neck. She looked beautiful.

"Hi," he said, at the sight of her instantaneously feeling the tightness in his throat.

"Let me put this in the icebox." He surrendered the bag with the Miller and stepped into the apartment. "Would you like one?"

"Sure," he said. "Great." While she went into the kitchen, he idled for a moment at a framed poster beyond the doorway. It was an ad for Allen Schweitzer's most famous movie, *Revved,* the story of a man, many other men, and a single beautiful woman. This was the director Reva had talked about at their meeting last week. He wondered what the poster was doing in Joan Wallin's apartment. When she returned with the glass of beer, he was afraid his hand was going to shake and took it with a studied slowness with both hands. She stood beside him now in front of the poster.

"*Revved,*" he said exploratorily.

"Yes," she said, gazing at the poster with him. "It's my favorite of Allen's movies."

"You know him?"

"Oh, yes," she said. "I guess we're sort of like

brother and sister, in a way. Come in, have a seat, make yourself at home. Please, be comfortable." As she said this, she moved into the living room at large, pointing out the sofa. She was charming, a gifted social entrepreneur—and the close personal friend of a psychotic movie director?

"Thanks, thanks," he said, smiling and moving into the living room. There was the black Roche-Bobois sofa and a big color TV. He paused at the floor-to-ceiling bookcase against the wall between the two windows, trying to get his bearings. He read over the titles on her shelves, hoping to slow down.

About to turn back into the room, hearing the honks of a momentary traffic ruckus below, he realized she was standing beside him with a glass of wine, surveying her own shelves of books. In the window to his right, he could see the lit thoroughfare of Columbus Avenue going on in the night. He took a swallow of his beer. She had the little original paperback edition of Kerouac's *Tristessa,* a book he had read and loved in high school. He turned to her, smiling. "This is a pretty place you've got here."

"Well, thank you," she said, looking up at him and smiling, but perhaps just a little nervous too. "Care to sit down?"

He walked over to the sofa, liking her being a little nervous. There was a white animal-skin rug between the sofa and the coffee table with the TV set on it. He sat down and then she sat on the other side of the sofa, catty-corner so that she was facing him, with one of her bare feet in front of her. She had painted her toenails a mat blue, though her fingernails were unpainted. He took a sip of his beer and put it down on the glass-topped coffee table.

"God, I'm just coming out of the stratosphere."

"You've been in LA..."

"Yeah—there and back in two days. It's a little dizzying."

She leaned forward and put her wine on the table. He caught a whiff of her perfume, a heavier, creamier scent than Betty favored, and at the same time glimpsed just an edge of a tan bra strap through the open collar of her shirt.

For the next several minutes, mostly catching his breath, he asked her about the Carlyle Bookstore and took a note or two down into his blue spiral notepad. At the same time, he watched her; the smile she had, the way her body moved as she sat. He was being the person he said he was. Things seemed to calm down. She laughed about the rakish septuagenarian who was her boss.

"Listen," she said as he was finishing a note about this man, "I know this is very rude and everything, but would you mind it a whole lot if we watch *Moonlighting?*"

"Not at all," he said, relieved.

"Oh, good. It's the only thing I like on TV and it just happens to be on right now." She reached up and switched off the black standing lamp beside her, darkening their corner of the room, and switched on the TV.

He had watched little bits of the show two or three times at home with the kids and Betty but never enough to know what it was all about. After a few minutes this time, he began to like it. He liked the guy, Bruce Willis, Cybill Shepherd's partner: Mr. Can-do, with a wonderful appreciation of his partner's charms. Then he started watching Cybill Shepherd. He liked him; and the two of them together; and then her.

"The thing about Cybill Shepherd," he said to her, "is that she's not really that pretty, but she can be really beautiful."

"Oh, she *is,*" Joan Wallin said beside him. "She really is so beautiful."

"Well, I think there are a lot of women that are better looking than her," he said, mostly to hear more from her.

After a long moment during which he wondered whether she'd heard him, she said, "But not that beautiful," and curled one of her feet further up under her on the sofa.

It was some sort of an opening. He turned to her, watching the slight changes of tincture on her skin in their darkened corner of the room as the scenes changed on the television. "Well, *you're* more beautiful than Cybill Shepherd."

She turned very quickly to him, said, "I am not," and turned back to the TV.

It was a nice answer. He kept looking at her, glanced at the TV again. The two were in their car together, making sparks fly. "Of course you are. Why do you think I started asking you all those questions at the Carlyle?"

"For your article," she said and glanced at him quickly again. Olive was the color of her skin.

"One reason. But you notice I didn't stop and talk to the logical guy: the last Confederate soldier from Big Sur at the front desk."

She smiled. Cybill Shepherd got out of the car at the corner, leaving her partner baffled at the wheel.

"By the way, what's your perfume?" he asked her. The beer must have been helping a little now, too.

"Paris," she said and kept watching the TV.

"I like it," he said and put his arm on the back of the sofa.

"Thank you," She glanced at him, smiled, and looked back at the TV.

The show was winding down. He took off his jacket and folded it and put it over the end of the sofa. He rested his arm again over the back of the sofa. Cybill Shepherd's partner had lightened his mood. He had also had another beer now. He moved his hand from the back of the sofa and rested it lightly on her shoulder. He waited for her to react but she didn't. Even if it wasn't yes, it wasn't no either. He looked at the way her hair fell in desultory fashion around her small, well-shaped ear with its pretty lobe.

"You have a pretty neck," he said, touching it lightly with the hand that rested on her shoulder. She seemed not to hear him. He moved over and lightly kissed her neck under the ear. She switched off the TV and turned to him.

"Why did you do that?" she asked quietly, her eyes steady.

"Because you have a very pretty neck," he said, holding back a smile.

"Oh," she said, not smiling, and continued looking at him.

He kept her eyes, and then, after a moment, came forward again and kissed her lightly on the lips; drew away for a moment, and then went back. She kissed him back this time, and each of them drew away.

"Thank you," he said, and smiled. He dropped his hand from her shoulder and leaned against the sofa. She watched him.

"What for?"

"Oh, I don't know." He put his hand on the back of her neck and pulled her lightly, testing, toward him and she let herself come down to him and they kissed lightly again.

They broke from this after a minute and she picked up his hand and kissed his palm. This was a jolt to him, to the feeling playing like a tide at the back of his throat. He had begun to be aroused but he didn't want anything to happen yet. He liked the feeling she gave him and wanted it to last a little bit.

"How come you're this beautiful woman," he asked her, "who lets me come up here and drink beer and watch TV, and play around?"

"Because," she said, looking at the air seriously.

"Because what?"

"Oh," she said, taking his hand again while still looking into space, "I thought you looked sort of familiar, and I liked your eyebrows. And then I found out you were famous."

He moved his hand away, interested. "You knew I was coming on?"

"Well, it only happens about a dozen times a day."

"And how many of them end up here?"

"You, and one other guy." She looked at him.

"Allen Schweitzer?"

"I told you—he's a friend. No, this was just a stupid thing when I'd just started. All men look at is your body, and since I..."

"Have a very nice one..."

"Thank you."

"Which reminds me." He sat up, moved her down against the back of the sofa, breathing in her fragrance.

He had his arm around her and moved his hand down her back. He could feel the push of one of her breasts through her shirt against his upper arm. The skin of her back beneath the shirt felt wonderfully soft. He held her for a moment, thinking he hadn't made out like this—not knowing what was next, or quite how to get there—since the days before he had met Betty, nearly twenty years ago.

She sat up and he let his arm slide from where he had held her. She stood up and walked to the windows and lowered yellow bamboo slat curtains. He looked at his watch. It was a little before eleven. He sat on the sofa watching her move, her light almost brittle movements inside the more sensuous cast of her body. She looked over at him from the window; he had gone down again, which felt better. He hoped he had the whole night in front of him.

"Would you like another beer?"

"I don't think so," he said. "Maybe we should take a walk or something."

"That would be nice."

He remembered how cold it had been. "Trouble is, I'm not dressed right. It's around forty degrees out there."

"I've got a sweater that would probably fit you."

"Great."

She walked across the room and opened a door beyond the sofa opposite the windows. He got up and followed her into the room.

It was quite small, with a neatly made-up king-size bed with a black silk cover, a telephone and a box of Kleenex on the bed table along with a paperback copy of *The King Must Die* by Mary Renault, a book he'd never read. Beside the bathroom door, on the floor, was a portable stereo tape deck. There were several tapes on the floor, including Marvin Gaye's *Greatest Hits*.

She went into the bathroom and he followed her. There was a black vinyl bath with a shower fixture. He caught sight of his face with hers in the mirror—his hair was wildly disheveled—and smiled. "What's this about my eyebrows?" he asked her in the mirror, his hand smoothing his hair.

"They're very adventurous," she told him smiling.

"That's because I'd like to make love with you," he said.

"We're going for a walk, aren't we?" she said looking back at him in the mirror.

"Oh, right," he said.

She walked out of the bathroom and he tried to further mold his hair into an approximation of its normal look. He needed the comb in his jacket pocket in the living room.

He walked out of the bathroom and she was wearing a black sweater with her white shirt showing below it under a black overcoat. She looked a little like the teenage girls in Connecticut, the layered look.

"Try that sweater," she said, pointing to it, a navy blue one, at the foot of the bed. "It's Allen's."

"I guess you two are sort of close," he said, putting the sweater on over his workshirt, standing beside her but not looking at her. She didn't answer. He didn't care. They were going to make love. The room's two windows, on either side of the bed, overlooked a courtyard with lit windows across the way. It was a Tuesday night on the Upper West Side. People hadn't gone to bed yet.

The sweater was an easy, slightly roomy fit, and he walked back into the living room. He put on his jacket and ran the comb across his hair a few times. She came out of her bedroom dressed up to go, the black overcoat now buttoned and the collar turned up around her neck. Very beautiful.

10

They walked through the late evening crowds on Columbus Avenue. He was about to steer her in for a drink at Ruelles when he spied through the picture window the back of a head that could have belonged to Sam McDowell, his former agent, and picked up the pace again. He was in the thick of it now, doing what most of his male friends who were married had done, at one time or another, but he had never before dared. (Anita at the Beverly Hills Villa didn't count—she had involved no effort of his own, falling literally into his lap.) He took her hand for a while, a lighter, slimmer hand than he would have guessed, continuing down the east side of the avenue until they had walked to the Broadway intersection. Across the thoroughfare, Tower Records looked closed and they turned around and headed back. They did very little talking, each absorbed by the night's pageant. It was as if the walk was another facet of foreplay, each of them testing currents that couldn't be put into words.

"Do you want to have a drink?" he asked her when they were within a few blocks of her building again.

"If you do," she said.

He loved the way she looked with her hair up. He remembered a crush he had had at Trinity on a Brearley girl named Sibyl Rutherford, who reminded him, and very likely herself as well, of Leslie Caron. Joan Wallin had something of that quality, too.

In the elevator, he kissed her again. Her mouth and skin were cool with the evening air. They got out at fourteen and she took her key out of her coat pocket.

"Don't turn on the lights."

"Okay," she said.

Inside the front door, he kissed her again and touched her face in the dimness. His heart felt wonderfully heavy with her, her air, her perfume.

"Let's go in, okay?" she said.

"Okay," he said and followed her in the darkness into her bedroom. The light from her windows—from the lit windows across the courtyard—gave the room a dim visibility. She took off her coat and hung it up in her closet by the bathroom door. He took off his jacket and put it over the top of a chair against the wall, and then removed the sweater and brought it to her.

She put it down on the dark, low-set bureau. She was letting down her hair and then began to brush it. Standing beside her, he held some of her hair to his face and inhaled its sheen. She was an orderly woman, and she was going to take off her clothes now and be naked for him.

She turned and kissed him. Slowly he unbuttoned her shirt, and when he was done, she took it off, and then stepped out of her jeans. He managed to unhook her bra strap as she faced him; she had heavy, shapely breasts.

"Take off your panties, too," he said; and she did. She had a heavily tufted black bush.

"What about you?" she asked, smiling at him in the dimness.

"I'm getting undressed, but I like to watch when a beautiful woman takes off her clothes. I'm a very sick man."

"That's not sick." She smiled and went to turn down the covers while he took off his clothes and put them on the chair. When he'd done this, he went to the bed and the two of them sat down on it. Her sheets were silk, black or very dark blue; it was too dark to be sure. He massaged her shoulders for a minute and then began to kiss them, and her neck. She smelled good, her actual body smell, like—what was it? A wet cardboard bakery? He leaned around and kissed the top of her arm and she said, "I have to do something. Don't go away."

She stood up and went quickly across the room and into the bathroom and shut the door before she turned on the light. He got up off the bed and went over to the tape deck and put on Marvin Gaye's *Great-*

est Hits, keeping it quite low, and went back and lay on his back across the silk sheets.

"Let me light a candle," she said when she reappeared in dark relief against the bathroom light, and then switched it off.

"That'll make two," he said, looking from her straight up at the ceiling again. She lowered the shades on the windows on both sides of the bed, and in a moment sat down on the bed by the bed table. He waited now, looking up, until her shadow loomed across the ceiling in the candlelight.

Then he felt her hands playing lightly along his legs, moving up lightly to the area around his cock which was half up again. He turned to see the Rigaud candle in its glass on the night table and then to her leaning over him. He put his hand in her hair and drew her to him while at the same time sitting up, and they kissed. In a little while, he lay back down again while she, still sitting up, reached down and lightly held his cock, her fingers rather tentative. Then she bent down and kissed its now burgeoning head.

When he let a finger run lightly along the lips of her pussy, there was a rush of her wetness. He moved down and kissed her smooth, soft stomach, burying his face in her softness, and then had an overwhelming urge to press his face into her thick bush. He did this now and, after a moment to acclimatize himself, started to taste her. She tasted like a combination of chicken, and—was it cardboard again? It was good. He began to eat her in earnest, getting heavily, compulsively, into it. He was lapping her, and at one point his lips smacked loudly. Very wet, she clenched her thighs around his face. Then she had him turn around without stopping what he was doing and he could feel her tongue darting around his cock, around and under its head. Then she was sucking him.

He moved his face from out of her black wet forest and said, "Did you put in a diaphragm?"

She took his cock out of her mouth and said, "Yes."

"If you do that much longer, I'm going to come."

"Oh," she said, and let go of his cock with her fingers, and sat up. "Don't do that."

"The thing is," he said, sitting up Indian-style and pondering his engorged member, "I've probably got more than one come tonight."

"Yes, but let's take our time, okay?"

She had such a nice, delicate manner combined with her erotic effluvia. They lay back down on the bed together and he put his arms around her. She was very light and very soft at the same time, like some kind of diaphanous substance of flesh. Then again, maybe he was losing his mind.

"We're in love," he said, smiling and watching the shadows on the ceiling made by the flickering candle.

"Mmm-hmm."

"I know you don't mean that," he said, her hair and face resting on his chest, "but I'm secure enough not to be devastated."

"I don't exactly do this with everyone."

"Yeah, but all it is, is the eyebrows."

"Well?" She giggled.

"That's okay, though, because I'm in love with your neck."

"You are?" she asked.

"Yes, we're going steady."

"I see."

He started playing with her arm, and then turned so that he could lick the musk of her armpits. In another minute, from above, he had entered her, his arms holding him up while she ran her fingers through his chest hair.

"You have the perfect chest hair," she told him.

"Thank you." He was very absorbed with his own situation: he picked up the pace a little, and she pulled her legs up and crossed them around his back. He continued his rhythm.

"Oh, God," she said.

He kept the pace for another minute or so, and then slackened off and tried a more exploratory, angular rhythm, going first to one side, then the other. Marvin Gaye was singing "I Heard It Through the Grapevine." Then she said something he couldn't quite make out. "What?"

"I want you to do me doggy-style for a while, okay?" she said, looking up at him.

This came as a small shock. It seemed such a breach in her style.

"Sure," he said and let her turn around and set herself on the bed on all fours, while he moved behind her on the bed and got up on his knees. She took him urgently then, inserting him, and he began again.

"Oh, God," she said.

She managed to reach around and play with his balls with one hand. Thrusting strongly now, he leaned over her back and began to play with her breasts, one in each hand, sometimes lightly scratching her nipples.

"Oh, God," she said again, and then: "Oh, please! Do that!" And as he continued his thrusting, she grew progressively wilder, twisting her back and raising her head to one side, letting it drop and twisting up to the other side, then down again, riding him harder and harder, her own rhythm taking over completely now, until she let out a kind of long whinny and, shuddering, came.

He held her for a while, still inside her, each of them on their side, curled wetly together, and winded. After a few minutes, he said: "Would you get on top now and dangle your breasts into my eyes?"

"Okay," she said, turning to look back at him, and smiling. In another moment, she moved around and sat up, her legs on either side of him, and settled over him slowly.

He braced himself up on his elbows and drew the two pillows under him, so that her breasts would be more accessible. He was playing with them lightly with his eyes, his face, his nose. She pushed them at him, and he licked some of her sweat off one. Then he held it and played with his tongue around the nipple which was stiff, wide and shallow. She pressed them at him again and he began to lick each nipple, groaning with joy. After that, he took as much of one breast as he could fit into his mouth and held it lightly, wetly, in a floating, liquid stillness.

She began to ride him in earnest, and he traded off for her other breast. She rode him faster and faster while he tried to maintain his liquid sojourn with her breast, and then she came to another shuddering, squealing halt over him and, after he released her breast, dug her nails into his shoulders for a moment and then let go and sort of melted on top of him. He lay under her weight, holding her.

"Did you come?" she asked after another moment.

"No."

"I didn't think so," she said.

But when he got on top again, her pussy holding him with an incredible, all-over grip, he knew he was about to come. "I want to come in your mouth," he said out loud suddenly, emboldened by her earlier request but still amazed at himself. At her bidding, he moved quickly over to one side and onto his knees. It was going to be over fast. She sat up and took him into her mouth but he stiffened.

"In your face?" he asked. As if an interior radar had finally lighted on a primary target, there was a sort of surge of assent in his groin. What was it about, though? Though it hardly mattered.

"If you like," she answered, very chicly he thought, and he went off instantly all over her face, and she laughed, licking the come at the edges of her mouth, and taking him into her mouth again for the last spasms of his jism.

Had he enacted here, perhaps, some kind of cumulative revenge fantasy, spurting jism in her face as he couldn't into Annette's or Lindy's? Yet she had not only taken it but behaved as if it were merely playful sexual etiquette. When she let him out of her mouth again, he found himself unexpectedly moved by what she'd done. He reached over to her night table and took a couple of Kleenex and, one hand holding up his head as they lay together, he gently wiped the rest of the come from her face. She licked his fingers while he did this.

"You're so pretty," he told her.

"But what about my problem?" she asked, smiling up at him.

"What's that?"

"I'm kind of a sex maniac, didn't you notice?"

Was that the situation? "Not to worry," he said and kissed the tip of her nose.

She smiled again. He moved off his elbow and lay flat on his back, looking at the ceiling in the candlelight. The covers were long gone off the bottom of the bed but he was wet with sweat, and hotter than July.

11

In the acoustic sparkle of the next morning, he walked down Eighty-first Street toward his car. It was a classic New York fall day, and he had just put Joan Wallin into a cab to work, and now he was walking back into his real life after his cosmic recess.

He retrieved the ticket off his windshield and got into the driver's seat, started his car, and pulled out into the morning traffic. He took a right on Seventy-ninth Street and came across a one-hour meter parking spot just before the corner of Broadway. On the spur of the moment, he decided to have breakfast before driving home and pulled into the spot.

At the newsstand on the other side of Broadway, he bought the new *Village Voice* and then walked up to Larry's near the corner of Eightieth, where the coffee was good. Sitting at a white marble table behind the front window facing Broadway, he had scrambled eggs and coffee and read some more about Daniel Ortega.

There was now duplicity, it occurred to him, on

both sides of the newsprint. He was an adulterer, reading an article about America's imperialistic foreign policy: in both instances, taking more than one's own. Yet, he could now employ a sort of psychic invisible shield beyond which he would simply not allow any thought to travel. He had done what he had done and seemed to need to do, and to get analytical at this point was moral ambivalence that was too little and too late to matter. Maybe he could get used to it.

On the radio in the café, he heard that a gridlock traffic alert was in effect since President Reagan was in New York for the UN celebration. James would drive home now and carry on as usual. There might be messages. Betty had perhaps done a new painting. Their children would be eager with precious gifts of their unfolding selves.

The house was empty when he arrived back that noon. The light of the rooms pleased him, and their order. Look what he had achieved with his long-term defection from the ranks of sober citizenry, his willingness to gamble with his life and talent (whatever it might amount to): he had achieved a quiet, attractive house. He walked into Betty's studio off the dining room and once more took in a fairly new fall landscape that was still on her easel: it was the scene from their front living-room window, the composition anchored by the round, black-painted stump of a branch taken off their big maple. It was a different light here, not as raw or hard on the eyes as the light of Northern California.

He went into his study and saw a note from Betty

that Reva and Henderson, his neighbor, had both called. He dialed Reva, turning in his swivel chair and propping his shoes on the old rolltop desk they'd found one afternoon at Yellow Monkey Antiques, across the New York border. He was in that brief, buoyant spell sometimes reached by staying up all night—as if he were almost as thin as air—and usually chased quickly by exhaustion. There was sunlight on his Italian shoes.

Later that afternoon, in a dream, he was confronted with a dangerous two-way door to a bar: he didn't know if someone was about to push through from the other side and he would be slammed on entering. He pushed through and found himself in a dimly lit enclave and took a seat at the bar and drank until his senses began to melt. He could hear President Reagan cooing softly over the radio in the background. He was aware of a terrible mistake in this indulgence. Everything depended on his sturdy mental purchase, his fundamental trust in his own sanity. The swinging door opened and in the bar mirror he saw Joan Wallin come in and he felt immediately gladdened and aroused by her presence. She stepped beside him but seemed to recognize him only partly.

"It's me," he said to her at the bar. "Just because I have a drink is no reason to think I'm crazy."

She smiled at him wryly and he woke with a start on the sofa in his study. The light had changed, darkened. He checked the time on the digital clock on the bookshelf. It looked like two thirty-one though he couldn't be sure and he wasn't about to get up to check.

If Reagan wasn't telling the truth about Nicaragua or about other things—like cutting back Medicaid and school lunch programs while proclaiming the young and the aged to be among his highest priorities—something sinister had infected the American air. It was as if the public sphere of the national life was in a state of static jam. Things were not flowing but rather were locked in sluices of movement around a hulking public falsehood. Was he now in his own person a smaller hulking falsehood? The thought made him stand up in the room and wander around, as if movement might sort it through. Then he left the room and went to the garage and brought his carry-on bag into his study. He closed the door again and unpacked his exercise book and went through the aerobics for day six on the room's buff-colored wall-to-wall carpet.

That evening he entered the upstairs bathroom and it was full of steam with Betty naked in the middle of it, having just emerged from the bath. She had a peach-colored towel around her hair.

"Hello," she said, smiling.

He had been about to shower and shave. They were going out to dinner at the house of people they barely knew. Her body, as always, distracted him. She was like a Tom Wesselman nude with the lipstick replaced by a natural rosy blush. Her nipples were extraordinary, her ass an Arabian ransom. An Arabian ransom? His life with her occurred in some proverbial South of his imagination, her body his perfect summer holiday. "Hi, where were you?"

"Oh, Tony has me running around for frames. They're giving me a *show* in December!"

"Congratulations!" He held her and kissed her. She gave him a very uncharacteristic French kiss. She usually wasn't this immediate.

"I've missed you," she said, and then ran her hand down over his fly.

This was practically unprecedented. He was their instigator. "You must be fertile."

"No," she smiled. "Well, maybe. Anyway, how have you been? Would you lock the door, please?"

Her radiance now seemed to encompass a blush. He went to lock the door and then returned to her. She unzipped his fly and took his cock out.

"Oh, I see you're fine." She smiled and kneeled down on the bath mat and began blowing him.

Hers was not, strictly speaking, a blow-job personality. Now and then, they passed through phases, but he couldn't recall anything similar to this. It also occurred to him that he had gone from Joan Wallin's mouth and into Betty's without an interval for the greater cleanliness. Betty was using her tongue now, too, and after several minutes, he was approaching his standing ovation, his third in less than forty-eight hours.

"Geez," he said, gasping and holding a towel rack for support, "to what...do I...oh—" and he was gone. She let him have his several spasms and even *mmm*ed at him while he did. Then she got up and walked to the Kleenex box on the back of the toilet and spit it all out into some tissues, which was more like it. "To what do I owe this honor?"

"Oh, nothing special," she said, barely restraining laughter. "I've just missed you."

"Sure," he said, trying to recover his breath. "What happens when I go away for a *week* and come back? Maybe we could get financing from Fox for that one."

"How'd it go?" she asked, taking over the sink and squeezing her hair through the towel.

The room's fog had diminished somewhat. "Pretty well. Annette's happy so that must mean something. How 'bout you? How's Tony?"

"He's okay. The show's a complete surprise, and I'm very nervous."

"It'll be great."

"I just want it to be *good.* She squeezed her hair in the towel over the sink again and then pushed it up over her head so it returned to its normal position. She was a great beauty, the best thing that had ever happened to him. He wondered if blow jobs could become a regular feature of their life together.

"Oh," she said, "I forgot to tell you. The Chasens are having one other couple tonight. Wanna guess who?"

"No," he said. He had forgotten to zip up and now did, although he was about to take off his pants. The fog had now all but cleared but the mirror remained clouded.

"Emery Rodefer and his wife. I think named Sally."

"No kidding?" Emery Rodefer was a good-looking broadcast journalist, known for his war-zone reporting. James had glimpsed him on Main Street in their town once or twice. "How'd you find out?"

"Ruth Chasen. She called to confirm this morning. I still can't remember who she is, but aren't you glad we're going?"

"I guess so. Maybe Emery knows what's going on in Nicaragua."

"Sure," she said, and put on her blue robe to leave. "Okay, have a good whatever you're going to do."

When they returned home around midnight, Marcia, their part-time housekeeper, got wordlessly up off the living-room sofa and was into her car before they had hung up their jackets. James undressed and got into bed with *Call It Sleep,* looking up from time to time at Betty's progress. She had put on a silk nightgown he particularly liked.

"God, that was odd," she said. "Mrs. Aquino had her husband killed?"

"That was crazy."

"I *know.*"

"He reminds me of Ray Ebert."

"Really? I couldn't think of two more unalike men. I mean Ray is a tree surgeon, isn't he?"

"So what? They both risk their lives for a living. They live by a certain code. They're a couple of rugged macho guys."

"So what? You're pretty macho when you want to be, too, you know?" She smiled and turned down the cover on her side of the bed and got in beside him.

He could smell her perfume but he had far exceeded himself and his eyelids were already drooping.

"Not the same thing," he said, and by a superhuman effort (to prove he was macho?) pulled himself up to put the book on the night table and switch off the light. When he got back down into the bed, she put her head on his chest and he held her. A couple of minutes later, in the darkness, he realized he was almost tired enough to go to sleep this way. Thank God for exhaustion: it put the cap on the hundreds of brain signals accumulated over the course of the day and said good night. By morning, or even the middle of the night, the army had thinned out: only a few dogged soldiers, your actual life, as it were, remained with their orders. The rest were gone.

"Darling?" she said.

He pulled himself up out of the half-dreamed soldier metaphor. Were dreams the work of a badly trained poet, a maniac of the mixed metaphor? And if they were, who could he call about it? Annette? His neighbor, Henderson, maybe? God?

"Are you there?"

Those, on the other hand, were real American words, gentle and entreating: ...*are*...*you*...*there*... Yes, those were good ones, very fine articles of sound, those.

"Yes," he said, as an afterthought.

Betty moved out of their snug arrangement and sat up and turned on the light, blasting his reverie into the room's dimensions. Here we are back in Connecticut, and this is your life.

"Oh," he said, and rubbed his eyes.

She had sat up Indian-style on the bed, facing him:

her breasts snugly tucked away in her nightgown, those two tucked in and all's right with the world.

"I...need to say something...Oh, darling, I've done something terrible and I have to get it off my chest."

"Sure," he said, closing his eyes again. "Just say it—it's okay." Sleep was what he was fighting.

"I went to bed with Tony Sears."

The words went into him like marbles in a pinball game, lighting up all his internal crossroads with sudden pain. "You *what?*" He opened his eyes, sat up and faced her.

"Don't..." she said, and then her face caved in, the mouth all crookedly out of whack, the eyes flooding red. "I'm so *sorry*...I'm just so..."

He was highly susceptible to her tears, but this was too much to swallow. "What the fuck are you talking about?"

"Don't *yell,*" she said between nasal blockages. "The kids are asleep."

She had always been a wonderful mother, even in the worst of their days in Septic Gulch. Now she was out there giving solace and succor to another man. Tony Sears, this blond, blue-eyed Englishman with all the social graces, had actually fucked his wife. He would have to beat the crap out of him.

"Tony Sears?" he said, incredulously. "Tony *Sears?*"

"He got me...*drunk,*" she said between gulps and gags. "He showered me with attention the way...*you* ...haven't done for years. It's been *your* career, not mine, just for years now. He gave me a new show and...everything..."

"I was trying to make money."

"I know. And you *did,* and I'm grateful. Look, I

did everything *I* could, *too,* you know, all those years ...Oh, it's just that I really *can't* hold my liquor and, he's very sweet and charming and he has this sunken living room..."

"Oh, right. His living room. 'My wife fell in love with another man's lobby, doctor. We had to get a divorce.'"

"I won't do it again," she told him. "He was terribly sweet but, I swear it, I'll never ever do it again. He likes you so much, James."

"He likes me? He likes me? That's really great. Maybe Tony and I can get together? Whatta we do now?"

"Nothing!"

"You fucked Tony Sears. You *fucked* Tony Sears. That's why I got the blow job, right?" He got up and took a blanket off the end of the bed. He could hear her sobbing again as he went downstairs to sleep in his study.

12

Children keep the world going, he supposed, driving Paul back from the doctor's the next afternoon, which was overcast and dreary. His son had stayed home from school with a sore throat and a light fever, and he and Betty had soberly decided to rule out a strep infection. So he had driven Paul over to have a throat culture taken. Paul was more subdued than usual, sitting quietly beside him in the front seat of the Mercedes while the radio played. Then, when he turned off Main Street, James heard his son singing along with Foreigner:

> I want to know what love is
> I want you to show me

He himself seemed as much in the dark as his nine-year-old boy at the moment, but it was Paul's unconscious high-pitched sincerity that moved him.

At home again, he got Paul back into his bed, kissed him, and Betty took over ministering to the boy, while James sequestered himself in his study. He looked at the notes for a new play he wanted to write, but had no appetite for it. But that being the case, what was there for him to do now? Maybe he could go beat up Tony Sears. Or maybe he could go fuck Joan Wallin.

Maybe he could do both.

Looking through the *Voice,* he discovered there was a lecture on the U.S. in Central America at the NYU Law School that afternoon at four. The speaker was Harvey Tride, the biologist and political radical. He knew he would learn something. He walked out of his study, put on his jacket, and called to Betty upstairs that he was leaving. She came to the top of the stairs.

"Where are you going?"

She was dressed in a brightly colored striped Ralph Lauren sweater, and a green skirt. She looked terrific. "I'm going into town."

"Okay—well, have a good time," she answered irresolutely, as if she wouldn't mind coming herself. "I'm...I told you, I'm..."

What—sorry? "Forget it," he said, interrupting her, and walked out of view and left the house and went into the garage. She had made it with Tony Sears. By a coincidence, of sorts, he happened to have made it with Joan Wallin, but that only confused the issue. It certainly didn't resolve it. He backed out of the garage and drove to New York.

"If you want to know what the Russians are all about," Harvey Tride told the crowd at NYU, "look at the

Eastern European countries. If you want to know about us, look at Latin America and the Caribbean."

Harvey Tride was a thin man of medium height dressed like a refugee from an old Bogart movie. As it happened, this was a look that was currently in fashion: the basic Banana Republic look. One could imagine him in some forties movie, a newspaperman sweating over his portable Olivetti in the jungle heat. The modest auditorium was packed with several hundred students along with a sprinkling of older radicals. He recognized Tuli Kupferberg in the crowd. The funny thing about Tride was that he reminded James of a WASP; his delivery was clipped and studded with ironic detail. What he had to say comprised a devastating indictment of American foreign policy from before the Russian Revolution (when the threat in the Dominican Republic was known as "the Hun") through the Kennedy epoch and into the Reagan years.

He quoted a top-secret directive from George Kennan, considered a dove, on postwar American policy to the effect that since we owned sixty percent of the wealth and were less than six percent of the population, we needed a way to make that fact palatable to the rest of the world. Enter the domino theory, etc.

We were, Tride said, a capitalist democracy, which wasn't a democracy at all. The major decisions were made in the private sector by the heavy investors, and the public was given the opportunity only to ratify those decisions at election time.

All this had a strange effect on James. He sat in the crowd, keeping his mind busy on the details of Tride's speech, and even took notes in the same blue pad he'd used at Joan Wallin's. But what was happening went beyond any particulars of Tride's information. The crowd was enormously attentive and affirmative, stopping Tride with applause when he said, for example, he wasn't sure Reagan even understood what he recited off the cue cards, and at the end rising in a standing ovation. It was like a sixties crowd, minus the drugs.

It was as if, suddenly, a secret history of their country was being told to them. Tride said it was extraordinary the way distinguished historians, effectively brainwashed, had not been able to write that history, but that that was another lecture. Standing up to go during the question period, James sensed that the suppression of that history was somehow at the heart of the boredom and inner restlessness he had felt in his father and struggled with in his own life.

It was the sense that American power per se was, both at large and in the most personal terms, a sad disappointment, an alienating and, in the end, sickening cul-de-sac. His father, an American millionaire industrialist, having invested his life in power, had ended up bereft of whatever might have given meaning or harmony to his last years. He was angry about his miscalculation but not willing to admit his mistake: he had put power before his family, his friendships, his own actual rewards. He had been sold a bill of goods. Sensing his father's impasse, James had begun, by his early teens, to search out alternative routes. In some still hardly fathomable way, it was a central fact of their lives that Tride was articulating.

* * *

"Hello."

"Hi, it's me. James." He was standing at an open telephone booth on the southeast corner of Washington Square Park. It was almost dark now.

"Oh, hi." She sounded happy to hear from him.

"Anything on TV?"

"*Hill Street Blues?*"

This was the program that followed his family's Thursday night lineup of *The Cosby Show, Family Ties,* and *Cheers.* He was in a different demographic sector now. "Are you free? Have you eaten?"

"I'm having dinner. You can come over, if you like."

"Can I bring you anything? Would you like some dessert or anything?"

"Not unless you would."

"Alright. See you in a while."

He had a cheeseburger and coffee at a Greek diner on Eighth Street. So what if it *was* sex, pure and simple? That wasn't necessarily a bad thing. Even Betty was partaking.

On his way to his car in the parking garage on Broadway across from Conran's, he stopped at a Greenberg's and picked up a little bag of brownies. Then he drove through the nighttime city to the Upper West Side. He put his car in a garage on West Eighty-third Street to avoid another ticket. He wouldn't be able to pick it up between two A.M. and seven the next morning, if he happened to want to go home. He figured he'd risk it. He walked down Central Park West and then took a right on Eighty-first Street.

She answered the door this time in a black sweatshirt and cut-off jeans.

"Hi," he said and leaned over to kiss her and entered the apartment. He gave her the bag of brownies.

"Oh, yum!" she said, peeking into it and smiling. "And I can make some whipped cream."

"Sure," he said. "But not for me."

Watching her move, he saw she wasn't wearing a bra under the sweatshirt and that her cut-offs ended way up on the thigh. She looked glistening, edible. He could feel his heart suddenly thumping in his chest. He made a circle in the living room, removing his jacket and draping it over the sofa, and came up behind her in the kitchenette and put a hand very lightly on her shoulder, as if mitigating against the sudden urgency of his desire. She turned, brushing a stray strand of hair from her eyes, and looked up at him.

"Hi," she said.

He kissed her and her mouth was already warm. He kept his hand lightly inside her hair. She began to French-kiss him, and with his other hand he got under her shirt and felt the soft flesh of her back. Almost immediately, she pulled the sweatshirt up over her head and was standing naked except for the cut-offs. Her whole body seemed enflamed. He smelled her perfume again, plus the under-odor she had, that cardboard odor of sweat, or sex, or both. He fiddled around and found the zipper of her cut-offs. By this time, she had her hand in his pants. He kneeled down on the kitchen floor and opened the breach and found her already wet. He pulled one of her arms so that she sat down on the kitchen floor, and began to eat her.

"Oh, God," she said, leaning back on the floor.

But this wouldn't be a slow, savoring occasion. He raised his head and pulled her cut-offs all the way down and off, and got himself out of his pants and into her. She lay under him on the red and white checked linoleum and started coming almost immediately, groaning and digging her nails into his arms and back. Then, breathing hard, he stopped himself.

"What about the diaphragm?" he asked.

"It's in," she said, holding herself forward under him.

She certainly wanted it. "You really need to be fucked," he told her, gasping, "don't you?"

"Yes," she said, out of breath too.

"That's why you weren't wearing any bra and your pussy was wet before I even touched you."

"Mmm-hmm," she answered, her face contorted under him, half smile half frown.

"If I came into the bookstore today, I probably would have had to fuck you on the floor of the shop." He gasped again. He was getting carried away and was going to come. He slowed up, letting himself rest on her for a moment.

"Come," she said. "It's okay now. Please come."

He began again, more slowly, his lust abated into a certain raw tenderness for this woman under him on the red and white checked kitchen floor. Now his cock expanded with some extra deposit of emotion he had kept back and, more slowly, more gently, they rocked back and forth until he reached his limit and exploded softly inside her. He felt a drop of sweat trickle down from his scalp and into his left eye. He kissed her above her breasts, and lay his head against her there for a moment while she held him.

Lingering over coffee at her oak roundtable the next morning, he heard a key in the door and looked quickly over at her. She was about to leave for work.

"It's okay," she said. "It's Allen."

The door opened and Allen Schweitzer came smiling into the sunny living room. He was a little taller than James—a full six feet, say, to his five ten and a half—and wore a black turtleneck sweater and dark corduroys with brown loafers. Curly-headed, he had a face that might have belonged to someone much younger: tan, even-featured and, just now, humorously animated.

"Good morning!" he said, smiling at them both, and came immediately over to James and shook his hand. "How are you? I hope Joan's told you how much I liked *London Bridge*."

She had in fact mentioned that they'd seen it together. "Well, thank you," James said, smiling and half rising into the handshake and then sitting down again.

"Yeah," he said, going into the kitchen and pouring himself some coffee, "it was great to see a movie about camaraderie and friendship and sex, without all the vile nasty other things I have to throw in to get financing."

"Well," James said, now looking over at Schweitzer as he drew up a chair, "I have to tell you the movie know-how there was ninety percent Annette Reed. You must know her."

"Of course. But she needs a script. Everybody has to have a script."

"Gentlemen," Joan Wallin said, standing up, "before you get too far into it, the working girl must leave for work."

He stood up and so did Allen Schweitzer, and they both saw her to the door.

"Gee," she said, "I feel like I've got a family here. If that doesn't sound too sick."

"We'll forgive you, babe," Schweitzer said.

James kissed her good-bye but felt a little disoriented by her departure. He closed the door, and headed with Schweitzer back to the table.

"Great girl," the director said. "And you must know how good you are for her."

"Really?" he answered, surprised by this and sitting down again and taking a sip of his now lukewarm coffee.

Schweitzer sat down across the table from him. "Oh, yeah. This means a lot to her. She meets a lot of schmucks. This is very nice for her."

13

Allen Schweitzer had a bold stride, and sometimes turned around and walked backward to establish eye contact when he made some point or wanted to catch James's response to something. Since he knew Schweitzer had to be in his late thirties, only a few years younger than he was, James was amazed by this display of energy at the same time he distrusted it. They walked along Columbus Avenue in the midmorning sunshine.

"You see," Schweitzer said as they passed the noisy grammar school playground on Seventy-eighth Street, "we had the same kind of father. Your dad's Redding Steel, right?"

"Right," he answered. "Or was."

"Or was, right. The steel industry really bought it. Those guys didn't keep up technologically with the foreign competition."

"Well, that was part of it. But he sold the company before that surfaced."

"Good move. Well, my dad made it in textiles. Same story, really. So we both got to go to Harvard, and freak out a little during the sixties, and make movies. When did your dad die?" Here Schweitzer turned around, walking backward, as if to catch James's response.

"'Seventy-six."

"'Seventy-six. Heart attack?"

"No, suicide. He got a very curable form of cancer and refused to have the necessary operation. He was angry about his life. He'd got the prize, you know, but it wasn't what he hoped it would be. He figured out a way to pretty much disinherit everybody while he was dying."

"No kidding."

Now a beautiful, athletic-looking black woman walked by in tight jeans and a purple jersey with a big white *10* stenciled on it.

"Yeah, ten baby," Schweitzer said, following her with his eyes. "You got it, babe; you and Bo, babe." He smiled and waved as James continued walking forward, facing Schweitzer.

"Chocolate princess," Schweitzer said, turning around and falling in beside him again. "Like Joan, you know."

"How's that?" The comparison didn't quite jell.

"Black women have soul, man. They're real tender. Like Joan, you know. They're not spoiled, like these Park Avenue fuck-arounds. Course it's a lot of fun to nail one of those, too."

"She really is a nice person," James said, feeling inane.

"And smart, too. You know how I met her? NYU film school. I was giving a screenwriting course, and she came in with this really tasty little script about growing up in East Orange and dating a black guy. Just like the Janis Ian song. Should be made."

"No kidding? She writes?"

"Writes like she fucks, man... Hey, listen. I apologize if that bothered you. We're not happening. For a while, but not now. I'm into younger women."

He must have gulped or flushed or something—Schweitzer wasn't exactly Mr. Sensitivity. They were passing an outdoor restaurant, buzzing with patrons and white-jacketed waiters. "*She's* young."

"Yeah, I'm talking younger."

"The interesting thing about pornography," the director offered an hour or so later, after they'd stopped for coffee, as they walked up Third Avenue, passing the huge high-rise co-ops of the East Sixties, "is that it's totalitarian and in that sense it's a reflection of what's happening here. What you see is a guy's idea of sex and sometimes they can find a chick who happens to corroborate the fantasy."

"Well, this radical, Harvey Tride, says there's no such thing as a capitalist democracy, anyway."

"Right on. Dig, whadaya think the movie business is about? I mean it's power and money and sex in very specific ratios: who sucks whose cock. Everybody's an unconscious totalitarian—like Annette Reed, for instance. You know, everybody's got this idea my movies are fantasies. I'd love to give them a tour of my professional life the last ten years and then have the verdict."

"So why do it?" James said. The early afternoon was balmy and full of little pocket breezes that happened and then were gone. They passed a high-rise's enormous circle driveway with a blue uniformed doorman at the front.

"Why make movies?" Schweitzer turned around here, walking backward, to take in James frontally again. "Because I'm a fucking wacked-out artist, man, that's why. And I'm betting when the smoke clears, they're gonna come back—if any of us are around, that is—and say, 'Hey, this dude got the idea what was happening.'"

"And what's that?"

"In the eighties? Come *on.* Sex and politics, sexual politics, political sex. Third World nations coming out from under the old missionary position, so to speak. Old imperialists softing off, and rolling over to take it up the butt. Look at these guys we've got up there now: they're scared Ortega and the others are going to gang rape them."

You had to hand it to the guy, he had his personal vision nicely squared away. Yet, now enjoying the conversation almost in spite of himself, James wondered whether he had any particular world view of his own, and if he did, whether it would fly with the likes of Schweitzer. By now he knew he had no real rapport with him. Schweitzer's entire persona seemed to be a predetermined strategy not for intimacy but rather for effective gamesmanship in, James supposed, the movie business.

"My idea," he started out with a deliberation designed to give him a moment or two to determine his exact direction while Schweitzer took up the stroll beside him again, "—my idea is to develop a kind of life rhythm." Like walking, maybe?

"Go on," Schweitzer said quickly, not about to dilly dally.

"Hey, Allen, you gotta let me have my rhythm here, okay?" Maybe he'd go for a charm gambit?

"All right, sure," Schweitzer said with an impatient smile.

"Okay, well, my life gets fairly complicated, it seems, round about now. And my mind is okay, but it's not my whole, or maybe even the major part of what I'm doing. But if I can breathe deeply and wake up each morning and go about my life and business without getting heavily self-hating and/or paranoid, I can more or less trust to the gods." He had a feeling he sounded dangerously like a refugee from an est seminar.

"Okay, but—well, that's maybe a little easy-come easy-go for me."

"Well, look, our dads brought home the big American dream, didn't they?" This, he hoped, upped the ante. There was a filthy homeless man lying asleep in the sunlight on the steps of a church at Seventy-first Street. He didn't know how much Schweitzer knew about his actual life and wanted to remember to skirt any incriminating details.

"Yeah—which is why we're gamblers, and artists."

"Yeah, okay"—James had begun to catch the wind here, he thought—"but doesn't it go beyond that? I mean we inherited their nervous systems, too, to a certain degree. My old man was bored and restless all the time. All he had to do was go to the office and kick ass. I mean, in the end, it seems like power is just this decoy, you know. It's not the real article. It's a *visual* solution, not a gut one. The only way out, as far as I can see, is actually finding ways to pay attention—or maybe instead of *paying* it, you know, on the capitalist model, just *giving* it away. Art helps. Beauty. The spring breeze, whatever. Friendship. I lived with my father, you know, and I picked up a lot from him that I need to work out and through, somehow or other."

"Well, but the way it turns out, he's probably not that bad an example for a movie director, you know."

Sure thing, Al. "That's true," he answered blandly, giving up. So Schweitzer loved his life. Fine. He looked up at the blue sky and noted a small perfect little white pillow of a cloud riding along, framed by the avenue. The planet was turning.

"Hey," Schweitzer said, "I wantcha to meet somebody. We gotta cut over to Park here."

They entered a building at the corner of Seventy-third and Park. Schweitzer was greeted by the Puerto Rican doorman and then they rode the new self-service elevator up to ten. Schweitzer rang one of three doors on that floor. In a moment, a tall brunette in a navy blue school jumper opened the door. She was what—maybe sixteen? She had a small-featured, intense, rather dark face and tousled dark hair. Her school uniform, James supposed, lent her a certain forbidden charm. School uniform, nurse's uniform—standard pornographic props. Something official and regimented beneath which lies a rosy bliss desperate to be released from its official entrapment.

"Hey, babe," Schweitzer said and kissed her. "Say hi to James. James, this is Marla."

"Hi, James," the girl said. "Come in."

"Hi," he said, smiling.

She ushered them into a large living room, heavily furnished with what might have been real Louis XIV antiques. The Sting album was playing. James sat down on the silk brocaded sofa and picked up a copy of *Manhattan* off a white marble coffee table and—as Schweitzer and Marla went out of the room—began to read a book review.

In another moment, the girl was back to ask if he'd like a beer. When he said yes and thanks, she went away again and came back in a moment with the beer in a glass and set it down on a big white linen napkin.

"Allen has to make a call. He says to make yourself at home."

"Thanks."

She walked out of the room again. In the break between songs on the Sting album, he could hear faintly through the open windows the traffic below on Park Avenue. He sipped the beer, finished the review, and reflected on the portrait in oil at the far end of the living room. The subject was a young blond woman in a white gown with a dignified yet rather mindless expression: like something beautiful somehow flattened under glass. At some point, it occurred to him that the glazed quality was in the woman's eyes, and that it could have been his mother's own look. Was that look, in effect, the flip side of his father's monomaniacal drive? He stood up, holding his beer, and walked out of the room and slowly wandered into and through the apartment's foyer, the dining room and the kitchen, all empty in the afternoon's quiet. Then he took a turn down a corridor and encountered open doors leading into a heavily furnished study and a bathroom. At the end of the corridor was a closed door, and he could hear Allen talking, either on the phone or to the girl. "Let him try it," he said matter-of-factly. "Just let him try it." James turned back toward the living room.

Sitting restively on the sofa again, he realized this apartment was not so different in style from the one he had grown up in, his father's Fifth Avenue duplex. Wasn't Schweitzer oppressed by the consuming, gaping emptiness of it? It was all James could feel in it. His life had begun in that vacuum. Now, having come through a period of poverty that had greeted him vigorously on the other side of his antipathy, it was as if he was looking out into the world for the first time. Somehow, the very engine that had roared in the rooms of his father's life seemed to be roaring through the silence here. He put his beer glass down on the napkin, and walked out of the apartment.

14

Driving home on the Saw Mill that afternoon, it occurred to him that maybe all any "artist" did was follow the contours of his period, and express them, willy-nilly, no matter what he might *think* he was actually doing. Betty and he had met during the sixties; that had been their time. Now he was buying the best albums of those years—*The Band,* Neil Young's *After the Gold Rush,* The Stones's *Let It Bleed*—and bringing them home to play for Lisa.

But only a few years ago, while they were still living in the drafty, half-converted barn in Marin County, it came to him that, sixties or not, there they were ensconced in the national capitol of the Me Decade, being suitably introspective, apolitical, and watching their diets. They even had Body Work for a while and went to the obligatory sauna afterward. Neither of them, however, had set foot in the epoch-making hot tub. A point of honor. Except they would have gladly done it if they'd been asked. The only thing that actually distinguished them from the mellow Marin crowd was the irrefutable fact that they spent the majority of their time each day juggling bodies, little ones: changing their diapers, cleaning their messes, feeding, clothing and otherwise taking care of them.

He slowed down for a red-haired, unshaven flagman about his own age with a road construction crew, who then waved him on through. He gave the man a friendly wave. This was civilization; one guy takes care of traffic flow; another guy tries to figure out the secret meaning of things to present it to the first guy during his leisure hours. That was the movies.

And then, even out there in Marin, something strange had happened. Well, it had been right around the time the seventies were ending. He and Betty had grown up in homes where the extras had been their apparent birthrights—private schools, trips to Europe, theater tickets; anything they really wanted, they got. That's what the sixties had been about: a bunch of spoiled kids taking the silver spoons out of their mouths and throwing them on the floor, along with the rest of the meal, the bib, the tray; and then turning the high chair over and kicking the governess in the ass and running out into the streets to find their worldwide counterparts. Wasn't *The New York Times* still trying to pretend it hadn't happened? These kids *didn't want* a piece of the pie. All they wanted was to stop the war, establish social justice, get high, listen to rock 'n' roll, party, make love...

Stevie Wonder was singing "Living for the City" on WPIX as James took the off-ramp for Route 35. The afternoon was beautiful; crisp and clear without being too cold. Both his nostrils had suddenly cleared. He leaned back against his seat, holding the wheel with one hand, and inhaled the svelte fragrance of the car's interior.

Rich kids, he and Betty had been, to all intents and purposes. So it had taken them about ten years to notice. Or maybe it was just that the times were changing again, everything turning around for the Reagan era. In any case, one morning he woke up in their converted barn and realized his closest neighbors were a doctor, a lawyer, and a building contractor. He and Betty were just getting by, driving a battered '67 Volvo and trying to meet the monthly mortgage payment and the grocery bill. His father would manage a grudging, imperious handout once or twice a year; and his mother a vitally needed Christmas check.

That fall Betty brought in a few thousand dollars with a show of her flower paintings in Beverly Hills. For a night they mingled in the fast track, and in the middle of the evening he found himself talking with a short, thickset man with whom he felt an immediate, easy rapport. At some point, it came to him that he was speaking with a Hollywood wunderkind, Oliver Hazen, the writer and director of a movie, *American Dimes,* he'd seen at the Montecito Shopping Center in San Rafael one summer evening; and come out of the theater feeling lighter than air.

"You know," he told Hazen the night of Betty's opening, "I enjoyed that movie more than any I've seen since *Blow-Up* in the sixties."

"It did pretty well at the box office," Hazen said, "but the reviewers went for my throat."

"And a few other things," his girlfriend, Terri, added. She was quite tall, pretty, and wore an "Annie Hall" jacket. The three of them laughed.

"Well, the thing I loved most about it," James added, "was that it really went the distance as a love story. It came all the way through the night right out into day."

Unexpectedly, Hazen seemed to pivot and draw into himself. Speaking as if to the floor, he said slowly, hesitantly: "This is something I've been thinking about. Some stories really are tragic and it's a mistake to shirk that off. I'd rather follow it all the way down, if that's the way it's going to go."

"The dark side."

"It's un-American," Hazen said and looked up at him with a half smile.

Now James hesitated. He had been writing plays for ten years, with a few productions off-Broadway and at the Magic Theater in San Francisco, and he was just then coming out of a depression that, though it had lasted several years, had yet had some healing element in it.

"Except sometimes," he said to Hazen, "there's a down cycle that turns out to be a melting and a turning."

Hazen didn't skip a beat. "Yeah," he said, "the Japanese have a word for it. They call it sweet sadness."

Sweet sadness. That was it, wasn't it? With that sweet, honey-tinged smell of fear in it. A red Porsche nearly side-swiped him and continued to do-si-do up Route 35. What's the difference between a Porcupine and a Porsche? The pricks are on the *outside* of the Porcupine.

*   *   *

The depression, he supposed, had turned out to be about—about just about everything. The end of the sixties (not really over until 1975 or 76), the end of the seventies (they lasted about as long as it took for the massage, the sauna, and the "rap session"), the beginning of the eighties—but most of all, perhaps, the end of his youth, that oblivious, glad go-power. And, not to forget, that little item Betty and he hadn't noticed for so long, being rich kids with cushions seemingly built in to their nervous systems—the fact that they were living in poverty.

During the sixties, of course, it hadn't mattered. It was even, for all intents and purposes, a point of chic. But unlike so many of their counterparts, they had committed themselves to a family and that made a critical difference. Suddenly they were looking straight into the realization that their own kids weren't going to get the same opportunities they had gotten. Forget the opportunities. There came a day when he couldn't scrape together the few dollars needed to buy Paul some new sneakers when his old pair were too small and in tatters.

Betty spent that summer feverishly painting for her show while he tried to take care of the children. That fall they had the opening, complete with an open bar and waiters with hors d'oeuvre trays, and he found himself talking with Oliver Hazen and realized he hadn't talked with anyone as interesting in years, maybe in his whole life, and he was *making movies,* for

God's sake. He had more money than James was likely to see in his lifetime.

When they got back home, it was as if the new era had been inaugurated overnight. Now in the middle of the night, he would wake up and not be able to go back to sleep for hours. One night, lying in the darkness, he realized he was sweating, although the nights were always chilly. Where was the money going to come from? If he wrote a hit play, an enormous *if,* he might make something. But how much? On the other hand, if he got a movie out, no matter if it were a hit or not, he would make real money. Hazen had given him his number at Universal, where he had an office, and told him to call and come out for lunch when he was in town again. As if he came down every couple of weeks. On the other hand, if he could write a movie he'd have a reason to go down and call and have lunch. His social calendar could sure have used the pick-me-up. Now, five years later, he was driving by a hillside rioting with the red and gold colors of fallen maple leaves, colors he'd missed, for the most part, for over a decade.

"Hey," Betty said to him one afternoon after they'd agreed he should write a movie, "better write about *before* we got here." Their town, a sixties enclave that had remained, despite all, a study in actively pursued downward mobility, seemed by then too far off the beaten track.

So he had come, in a roundabout way, to *London Bridge,* which he imagined out of their adventures with two friends on a six-week trip to London when Lisa was a year and a half old and they all still dreamed of turning the world on its head.

London Bridge at twilight and not too many American Express traveler's checks left. He had invented his old East Coast pals as latter-day yuppies just before they settled down, the last fling of youth. Writing the movie those mornings in their back bedroom, looking out from time to time at their California garden, was the most fun he'd had writing in years. Suddenly, it seemed to be working.

When he'd finished the first draft, he managed to sublet a one-room studio apartment in Beverly Hills for two months—September and October—and move down to see if he could sell his script. He had the first-floor apartment in a small, two-story building on McCarty Drive. He had made a list of contacts, and friends of friends, and systematically put in a call to each. Naturally, he'd called Hazen the moment he'd arrived in town, but he'd missed his chance: the director had broken up with his girlfriend and moved to New York. Sitting at the kitchen table, James drank many cups of coffee waiting for his calls to be returned. He listened to the people walking across the floor upstairs. He watched the sunlight advance and recede on the little alley-driveway beside the kitchen window. It was a very quiet neighborhood.

The actress from whom he was subletting got a call one morning that he picked up, and it turned out to be an actress he'd known years before in New York, Trudy Winslow. She had played a role in his first play, *General Electric,* which had been produced at La Mama, and she was now in a TV series. He asked if she knew anyone who might be interested in his project, which he described, and she recommended he call a producer at MGM, Harvey Tilden. It turned out to be his first real break.

He called Tilden and was invited to deliver the script to his house later that afternoon. He said he knew of James's work but didn't mention anything by name. The house turned out to be quite lovely, though not large, nestled on a hillside high up in the Hollywood hills. Tilden was fiftyish with an overly manicured air. He was house-proud and also wife-proud, his wife being ten or fifteen years younger than he, a large, bookishly attractive woman named Martha. James and Tilden spoke for a few minutes, sitting in the living room, which had been decorated in the French Provence style, all unfinished wood and dark blue and white fabrics.

"I'll read the script and call you tomorrow," Tilden told him at the door as he was leaving. It was a line he'd heard about a dozen times by now. Usually, he never heard from them again: studio executives, independent producers, directors and several movie stars. Tilden called that evening just after dark. James was lying on the bed, reading *The Great Gatsby* and thinking about going out for a cheeseburger. The phone rang and he picked it up and said hello.

"God, *London Bridge* is wonderful."

He immediately recognized Tilden's overripe voice. He sat up on the bed, discarding Gatsby and Daisy and Nick Carraway. As it turned out, Tilden wasn't able to put together a deal, but the fact that he optioned the script constituted James's official entree into the business.

15

That night in Connecticut, at dinner with Betty and the kids, it was as if a certain rhythm, at this point a kind of alternating current in his life, grew palpable.

"You guys," Lisa said smiling at Betty and him, "Stephanie has this idea that when I'm nice to her, it's because I feel sorry for her because she looks terrible. And when I'm mean to her..."

"When you're a *bitch,*" her younger sister interceded loudly, smiling.

"...When I'm a bitch," Lisa continued, "when I'm a bitch, it's because I'm jealous that she looks so great. So after she told me that, I said to her, 'Okay, Stephanie, well how do you think I think you look right now?' And she said, 'Gorgeous!'"

Though he'd been trying to maintain a certain remove in Betty's presence, he cracked up laughing at this, and so did she across the table. After they had taken their plates into the kitchen, the rhythm carried over into the living room. It was Friday night and the weekend loomed comfortingly, he knew, for the kids.

Paul was down on the buff-colored living-room carpet with his stack of Garbage Pail Kids: Clogged Dwayne, Art Gallery, Wrinkled Rita, and the like. He had stayed out of school again today, but it looked like he'd be ready to go back by Monday. Stephanie was curled up in a chair reading *Smart Women* by Judy Blume. Lisa put the *Stop Making Sense* album on the stereo, giving James's mood a percussive underpinning. Betty was in the kitchen putting the dishes in the dishwasher as he got a fire going and then sat down on the sofa with the last part of *Call It Sleep.* Had he called it that because that was the condition of his immigrants, a waking sleep? Lisa now had the entertainment section of *The New York Times* spread out in front of her on the carpet a few feet from where he sat.

It was a mood that had come over him once or twice in Marin, too; again, as he remembered, in the after-dinner wind-down: the dance of all their identities suddenly attaining a sort of perfect equilibrium, a transparency. The sentences in his book and the backlog of the past week or so vied for his attention, splitting it, and leaving him momentarily thoughtless in the middle of the living room's festive ambience: his children, these growing things; this music; this night. Still, there was his actual life.

Allen Schweitzer had proved surprising, and then disappointing, hadn't he? Someone with very nearly his exact background trying to parley that vacuity into legend. It just didn't make sense. On the other hand, here he sat, maybe just a bit too snugly, doing what?

Betty breezed into the room wearing jeans and the black sweater that so complemented her blondness.

She smiled at him, but he wasn't having any of it. She sat down beside him on the sofa and also seemed to regard the living room for a moment, as if she too had caught the mood: there they both were, then, observing a room filled with the varied designs of their progeny. Maybe, in the end, a lot of what they were now had to do with the fact of their family: it had moved each of them off the pivot of self, so to speak, and made them each join in the ancient tour of duties known by all parents. Jump down, turn around, pick the baby up and change her. Back out the car and go pick up groceries, gas and a pizza to go. Feed everybody, make sure there was heat enough. Light enough. Books. Music. And then see what ensued. It was another you, another me, and the two of them, after a decade and a half of this, were like edgy veterans who had just crossed some epic threshold and been rewarded with a rather dizzying change of circumstance.

Success, they called it.

So he felt compelled to go after someone else's flesh? So she did? Who could explain it to him? The phone rang and he got up.

"Hello."

"Where have you *been?*" It was his neighbor, Henderson.

"Hi, Rick. Complications. How are you? How's the sound system?"

"It's—*here,* for Christ's sake. This is compact disc I'm talking about, by the way. Have you eaten?"

"Yeah, we just finished." Betty was looking at him from the sofa, wondering what was up, but he kept his eyes averted. He was punishing her, a completely ridiculous stance, as he was only too aware, but then what of it? He had his limits just like any other man.

"Look, wind down with the kids for a while. It's the weekend, damn it all, and then stop by, if you feel like it."

"That would be nice, Rick, thanks."

"Bring Betty, if she'd like. Mary's about."

"I'm not sure what she's doing."

"Whatever."

He said good-bye and walked back and took his seat in the living room. Betty put her hand on the back of his neck and let her fingers play through his hair but he didn't respond and she eventually took her hand away.

In his car that evening he drove to Main Street, and then south to Rick and Mary Henderson's white colonial that sat next to the Catholic church. He had heard a good, tight sermon there on Easter Sunday their first year in the town, and seen the minister since at Stop & Shop, an upright figure with that pink flush that seemed to flourish among clergy. At night Main Street was black and white and various grays, with tiny fluid incidents of real color, mostly greens. He took the long driveway off Main Street and parked beside Mary's pale blue BMW. Rick had his black Jaguar in the garage. James walked to the Hendersons' lit entrance and rang their two-clang chimes.

Rick opened the door wearing a black *Rolling Stones Tour '65* T-shirt and a pair of jeans, smiled and led him through the foyer down the stairs to the rec room. Five or six years older than James, he was something over six feet tall with a powerful, now slightly fleshy body. Since James had last seen the wood-paneled downstairs, straw matting had been layed over the whole floor, and bookcases and director's chairs added, as well as a large knotty pine coffee table in front of the wine-dark upholstered sofa.

"Beer?" Rick asked him from the small bar in one corner.

"Place looks great," James said, sitting down on the sofa. "No thanks."

"Oh? Cleaning up, are you?" Rick popped the cap on a Budweiser and sat down on a red director's chair opposite the sofa.

"No, just not thirsty."

"Well, Mary's brother sent me some Dunhill cigars, so think about that for a minute. What have you been up to?"

"Listen, I'm sorry. I've been going through some kind of minor life crisis or something."

"No kidding?" Rick hadn't shaved and his reddish stubble was flecked with white. He drew on the Budweiser and looked back at James as if squinting. "Oh yeah?"

"Yeah, I don't know." James was looking at the poster of a maroon Rothko on the wall beyond Rick.

"Cheer up. Mary flushed my grass down the toilet. Anything that survived in our septic tank is sitting pretty, I can tell you that. Here. Check this out." He got up and inserted a CD into his sound system beside the bar. Piano, bass and drums came on with a clean fidelity that surpassed anything James had heard beside a live performance. "Bill Evans," Rick told him, sitting down again. "Scott La Faro on bass."

"Hey!" James said. "Three-dimensional sound."

"Isn't it hot?" Rick said.

They listened to the first track before saying anything again. Then James began to talk to his neighbor, with whom he'd visited three or four times over the past year, and with whom he felt, as with Oliver Hazen, more rapport than any actual visit might have warranted.

"I guess part of it is being successful, quote unquote, for the first time," he said as Rick took his seat again after lowering the volume, "although the more I think about it the more I realize I'm all slightly out of kilter. The movie business definitely can do without my type. So if I want dough, I'm going to get my ass kicked as part of the bargain."

"Big deal, join the club," Rick said to him smiling. "What's the alternative?"

"Basically, I figure—"

"Listen, a cigar?"

"Oh—sure, great."

His host stood up again and went to the humidor that sat at one end of the bar and brought back two cigars and sat down and began to cut their ends with a small silver instrument, holding each cigar over a black glazed ashtray on the coffee table.

"Anyway," James went on, "after this next thing, I've got to let it buy me some time. I've got a play I want to write and I damn well better write it unless I'm planning on selling my soul for this—"

"Riot of pleasures?" Rick said, grinning up at him.

"Well, you know as well as I do."

"Oh, I'm older than you are, and I don't mind a bit. Not a bit. I got carried away with the marijuana, I guess, but I've never even *tried* coke, and believe me it's not for lack of opportunities. Frankly, I've had enough of all that already. Why get involved with a new problem? And I'm planning on settling down again soon to—to just write my usual, you might say."

There was a drum solo happening now.

"Well, I'm beginning to notice that if I don't work I don't have enough to do, and then I can get into trouble."

"Men are lonely fuckers, and that's a fact."

James took this remark in, smiling, and then asked, "But how do you like this compulsive number that's going down now, you know? These people don't have lives, just careers. Period. And they run around with this fucking intensity... Women too—not just men anymore. In fact, women are my *bosses* now, for the most part..."

Rick held a cigar out to him. James put it in his mouth and Rick held a match to it until it was lit.

"This whole country," he went on as Rick lit his own cigar, "I mean, do you get it? I don't. I want to write a play about the Stalinist period in Russia. It's very interesting. Just thirty years of nightmare. Thirty *years*. And somehow people like Pasternak and Akhmatova and Mrs. Mandelstam kept some kind of perspective while everyone else went mad or was murdered."

"It's not hardly comparable, though, is it?" Rick asked, leaning back in a cloud of smoke.

James was surprised by the mildness of his cigar. "These cigars are good."

"Yeah, I think my brother-in-law's got me hooked."

"Well, it's a lot subtler here, that's for sure," he said, returning to Stalinist Russia. "But look around. What are we doing in Nicaragua? What's Reagan doing?"

Rick shrugged. "Same as always. General Electric got the guy they groomed to be president. AT&T probably have the same big plans for Cliff Robertson."

"So maybe I'm waking up. I heard this talk, this radical, Harvey Tride, says we live in this country—and he's talking about *us* here, the privileged middle-class—as disenfranchised morally as the people in our colonies (including our ghettos) are economically. Then you read a book like I'm reading now, *Call It Sleep,* about the Jewish ghetto on the Lower East Side at the turn of the century, and here's this guy mining the deepest levels of the whole immigrant story. Our parents, in other words, more or less. But the book requires a *reader,* not a guy in a beach hat who's made it. I don't want to lose it, not that I'm sure I ever had it."

"What the hell are you talking about?" Henderson said to him now, smiling. "I haven't understood a single word you've just said. My father sold insurance in Maryland. He failed as a *WASP,* goddammit. Many do. You want to write a play, nobody's stopping you. You want to be unhappy about making a few bucks, or thinking you're a prostitute or a gigolo or whatever, no one's gonna stop you either. As Yogi Berra said, 'If the fans don't wanna come, nobody's gonna stop them.'"

"What have you got to drink?"

"Beer? Whiskey?"

"Beer."

Henderson went back to the refrigerator and brought back a Budweiser, popped the cap, and put the can forward on a dark red coaster on the coffee table. "Look," he said, "I'm not saying it doesn't make me nervous: the money, the lunches, the options, including pussy—none of that was exactly my métier up to now. And, okay, go ahead and freak out, if it'll do you some good. Well, here: let me show you how it comes down in one house, okay?"

"Great," James said, smiling.

After Rick had gone upstairs, James took a sip of his beer, set his cigar down on the black glazed ashtray he was sure one of Rick and Mary's grown-up children had made in grammar school, and walked to his friend's bookcase. He looked over a shelf of Ross McDonald's books, and just above it, a shelf of Elmore Leonard's. He heard Rick coming back and walked back to the sofa.

"Okay, sit down and check this out."

James took his seat and Rick handed him a framed color photograph of a young woman with blond hair and a certain intensity in her kittenish features. He held the framed photograph and then asked, "This is?"

"Linda," Rick said, in his chair now. "She's at the University of Pennsylvania this year, a freshman."

"She's a beauty," he said, setting the photograph down on the coffee table.

"Well, it's like this," Rick said, picking his cigar up from the ashtray and puffing on it before he continued. "And since I've got a few years on you, you might want to listen up. These people we're living with, and we're sweating for, and I'll go so far as to include (just for the sake of argument) selling our souls for: these people who begin and then grow up inside our lives, and whom we fight with and kiss good night, and take to the beach, and recommend good books to—these people, pal, don't stay *forever.* That's the kicker, take my word for it. They are, in a manner of speaking and all evidence to the contrary, God's gifts to our lives. And when they leave, take my word for it, it ain't that easy. Now this person you're looking at there"—he gestured to the photograph—"that young lady was, is, and in some way always will be, the light of my life. I got to watch her grow. I saw creation up close, intimately you might say, for eighteen years. And it was, with all the other factors figured in, still a great thing to see, a heartening thing. And it also may have just kicked my ass enough to get me through everything else."

"You and Mary must really miss her and—the other kids." James, who wasn't good at remembering names, had seen one of Linda's two older brothers once: a sturdy young man helping his father prune a tree one afternoon in their front garden.

"Oh, yes. Yes, we do indeed. After all, the big thing about living this way, being married, having a family, doing our work, and so on and so forth, is this. Your life has a goddamn *design:* I mean to see a new thing through into a young thing and then see it take its place in the world. My lord, that's the damn song of the ages."

"I agree," James said seriously, nodding. His friend's passion was both unexpected and a touching corroboration of the mood that had come upon him after dinner that evening; he was glad, just then, to have him in his exact neighborhood of the world.

"And look," Rick went on, "Reagan tells lies. And Reagan may not even know or care that he's lying. He may not be the smartest guy in the world—he comes from a broken home himself, after all, with an alcoholic father—and the guys he works for may not be too bright either. In the long run, we know they're not. And *The New York Times,* which set me up on easy street, isn't exactly incorruptible either. But so goddam what, you know what I mean? Because I'm just a craftsman and I'm on the planet for so long and I've had great gifts given to me by my wife, and my family, and my work."

"Well, still," James said, leaning back in his chair, "there *are* all the people all over the world who are holding us up here by the sweat of their backs."

"I agree. And I have to and will do *something* about that. I'll send my money to Guatamalan Refugee Relief and Amnesty International and El Salvadoran rebels and wherever else I figure it should go. I may even go down there to Nicaragua with a group of other concerned, suitably apologetic citizens. And I'll send my money to the hopeless Democratic party. But what I'm saying is this. My real life is closer to home—being a grandfather is what's going now for me—and I can't not value it, and not take some care and pleasure in going about it. Because if I do, I'm not going to be of very much use *after* the revolution, see, and that's when I always hoped to shine." He smiled here at James.

"Amen," James said, smiling and drawing on his cigar.

16

Waking from an afternoon nap in their room, he gazed from his pillow at the willow tree at the far end of the garden. Two birds were at the top of it: one at the apex, the other to the right and just below. The one at the top would make a three-note call; the one below would answer with a single note. James had a clear view of the lower bird, and to make his single note utterance the bird's whole body was engaged—beginning with a downward thrust of his head. He watched him execute his note three times, following the three-note preamble of the higher bird. Then there was silence. It was as though the lower bird was waiting for his precursor notes to recur—but they didn't. Then the top bird flew away, and the lower bird flew after it.

Something in his afternoon dream had hurt him, so that he woke with his throat choked but his eyes still dry. These tides he lived inside of seemed to have their own laws, advancing and receding with no particular regard for his worldly circumstance of the moment. The dream had to do with Lisa. She had been taken away from him, been killed or lost somehow. And he had told someone that if that's what it came to, there wasn't much left of him. He didn't know how he could cope with the pain of such a loss: his clear-sighted daughter. He would bear the pain, perhaps, but only as an automaton.

Now it occurred to him this was about his talk last night with Henderson, who had lost his daughter to her adulthood, and yet still felt the loss deeply. What a simple thing a person was, in the end, at least in the matter of the affections. An attachment occurred and it was no easy business to unattach.

It was as lovely out this window as it had been out the back bedroom window of their drafty Marin house, with its view of a huge, stately eucalyptus. As the years had gone by in that house, he had grown attached to the tree and even thought that he would like to be buried under it. The sunlight in the willow, the smell of the garden wafting through the open window. Who do you love? Tell me who—who do you love? And what? The fact was that talking to a solid, centered man like Henderson did him good. Here was someone trying to chart a course with a certain decency and humility. There was work to do. He himself should find it. Begin his play, for instance.

He sat up in the bed, his blood reorienting for a moment in the change of position. He was an older thing now as people went. Something seasoned a bit by at least a couple of the major storms his circuits would be required to weather, barring an all-out nuclear holocaust. Maybe the Russians or Qaddafi or somebody would press the big button and everything would go to ash: he himself, ash. The ash standing like a man for a moment, and then, at the slightest breeze, keeling over into thousands of particles: his stories, ideas, his affections too.

At an early spaghetti dinner that their housekeeper, Marcia, made, they were all caught up in remembering Marin again, a mood half elegiac, half comic.

"Who was that violinist who was supposed to be gay, remember?" Lisa asked the table at large, turning to him at last. Of course he would miss her. She had a certain dispassionate affection for the things of this world—like a scientist, he imagined.

"You mean Steve Chase?" he said, recalling a blond man around his own age, a classical violinist known locally for his recitals at Mrs. Florentine's Sunday garden parties.

"Oh, *he* was cute," Betty said at her end of the table.

This set Stephanie and Paul into rollicking, disheveled glee. "Mom loves him even though he's gay!" Paul chortled, and Stephanie went into a silent paroxysm of laughter.

"You know," James said, "I once saw him jogging naked on Clearwater Road."

"Really?" Lisa said.

"Really." He had passed him in his car, at the time mercifully not familiar enough to need to wave. It was a measure of that period, the unbridled Me Decade, that he remembered feeling rather glad for Chase to have made this bold personal breakthrough: jogging with no clothes on for anyone who happened to drive by to see.

Now the phone rang and Paul quickly moved out from his chair to answer it while at the same time saying broadly, "That's why he was known as..." and here he picked up the phone: "...Penis! Hello." To whoever was on the other end, this would have to have come out: "Penis! Hello." They were all laughing, and Stephanie was down for the count, virtually below the line of the table in silent hysteria.

"What?" said Paul. "She's here. Just a minute." Holding the phone, he said, "Lisa, it's for you."

James and Betty looked at each other directly now for the first time in several days. Lisa took the phone from Paul.

"Hello...Oh, *hi,* Michelle. Listen, let me get the other extension, okay?" She put down the phone and went upstairs. "Okay, you guys," she yelled down to them from the other phone, "hang up now."

"You're deadline worked," Betty said to James after hanging up.

"Well," he said, "she didn't even have to make a call," and got up to take his dinner plate into the kitchen and get a cup of coffee.

In their room that evening he told Betty he had to be in the city that night to meet with Annette Reed and that he might need to stay overnight. Annette Reed was in California. Betty seemed to have resigned herself to some kind of penance, as though she had brought upon herself whatever attitude he assumed.

"Are you having an affair?" she asked him quietly as he was putting on his jacket to leave. There it was, the question he had up to now averted. The sun had gone down and he had pulled the shade beside their closet and switched on the lamp on the table between their windows.

"No," he answered and stared absurdly forward into the dark closet.

"You better stop soon," she said. "I have."

"I said, no, I'm not," he said, and turned and looked at her standing beside the bed in jeans and a dark blouse.

"Are you in love with her, or what?" She made a small smile.

He sat down in the blue upholstered chair by the window, letting go with a heavy sigh. "No," he said, "I'm not. But I don't hate her and I don't want to hurt her. This whole move just seems to have shaken me up."

"Finally!" she said, looking at him openly and without, so far as he could see, malice. "I've been waiting for you to say something about all this since it started. We used to talk every day when we had no money. Then, when we got some, that *stopped*—like everything was supposed to be perfect."

"You know that tree in our yard?"

"Here?"

"No, at the old house. The big eucalyptus."

"Sure."

"I used to think about being buried under that tree. I mean I was in my thirties and I was really thinking—and not in a sad way either—about dying and being buried in that meadow."

"We were sort of buried alive out there, I guess."

"Yeah, maybe," he said, sighing deeply again in the chair. Yes, they used to talk; this was an old engine of their lives that was turning over again. "Now we've gotten out and things have gone a little—haywire, I guess."

"They do!" she said. "You don't read magazines, but I do, and they go wrong like this all the time—success, failure, moving to a new place, midlife crisis, and this all has to be multiplied to a higher power for people who free-lance. I mean when an executive moves, the company moves him. But we talked before, and now we don't anymore." This last word she swallowed and he knew she was close to tears.

He stood up but couldn't quite go to her, still standing beside the bed, and turned toward the window again and then moved to the other lamp on the table against the wall opposite the closet and switched it on, too. "I'm sorry... I didn't know what was going on exactly. All these details..."

"Oh, I know. Sometimes I wish we could go back to one room."

"And the other thing is—" He turned back to her again. "It's not like our parents are around to help out." Betty's parents had retired to London. His own mother, for years an alcoholic whose only exercise was compulsive shopping, had died two years before in her sleep in the Greenwich house at sixty-five. But even when they'd been available, none of them had shown much interest in being grandparents. "I don't know. I think part of the trouble is there are so few real families around. Kids are goddam accessories, like expensive pets, you know? 'Brad and I have decided to complete our lives. This spring I'm looking forward to insemination.'"

"Well, *we* did it *backwards*." Betty had lain down on the bed now with her head resting on the big blue-patterned Pierre Deux pillow. "Everybody gets their career together and then has..."

"Yeah, *one* child. Did you ever know an only child?"

"You."

"Me, right."

"You're not so bad," she said.

"Listen, I've got to go in tonight," he said, standing indecisively now in the center of the room. "You've got to—just trust me. Just give me another twenty-four hours, okay?"

She sat up now. "What's going on? You know Tony and I have stopped—friends. But if you want to get a divorce and marry someone else, you've got that choice. Is she married?"

"No—but will you take it easy?"

"Take it easy?" She stood up now. "Look, James, you do what you want, but I'm not sitting around in limbo for weeks and months and years while you have some affair." Now she started to shout. "Do you hear me? I've worked too damn hard for that all these years!"

"Look, the kids are going to hear this. I have to go somewhere tonight, that's all. I'm trying to do the right thing here."

"Sure you are," she said, looking at him, her face flushed with anger. "I can just see it."

In the car, with other mobile citizens ahead of and behind him in their cars in the darkness, it occurred to him that his life now took place in a sort of bubble of accessories, a sort of oddly comforting isolation chamber: like the Mercedes itself. But he was no Henry David Thoreau, either, and then again that seemed only the flip side of the same thing. It *was* the family, so far as he had experienced, that provided the way out of loneliness and into some cognizance of the ways of the real world. There were other ways too, he supposed, but he just didn't happen to know what they were.

He used the same parking lot on Eighty-third Street, without giving it a proper moment's consideration. He was a creature of routine, familiarity, the long haul ingrained in his being as a daily thing. That was his métier. Not really the right kind of guy for a casual affair. He wanted to get comfortable in his surroundings more than he sought novelty. Success perhaps allowed him an opportunity to play the sexual imperialist, but he wasn't playing it well. Why had he told Betty about it at the moment he knew he was going to end it? Because a lie was too uncomfortable? Or was it part of a generic revenge on, in Betty's case, the very woman who had stood by him and encouraged him when they had nothing.

He had called her before he left from a public telephone in the shopping center. She answered the door now wearing the clothes she had worn on the first night he'd seen her: the jeans, bare feet, and loose men's white shirt on top.

"Hello," he said and kissed her and moved into the living room. She followed him to the sofa and sat down on her end and smiled in a slightly heavier way than he remembered.

"Guess what?"

"What?" he said, studying her as if to determine what it was that had changed about her.

"I'm stoned."

"Really? What on?"

"Oh, just some grass. But I shouldn't say 'just.' It's some of that sticky stuff, you know, that's all male or all female, I can't remember which, it sort of pokes these holes all through your brains."

"Sinsemilla?"

"Right! This gay guy at work bought some and he gave me an envelope for twenty-five dollars which is supposed to be very cheap. You look beautiful, by the way."

"Well, thank you," he said, smiling. Her personality had changed too. She didn't usually say things like "You look beautiful."

"Want some?"

"Uh—no. I don't think so."

"Oh, but you've *got* to," she said.

"Why is that?" he said, smiling again.

"Because it's very sexy, and I want to watch television and stuff..."

And stuff...Something told him his timing was off on this sober proprietary mission. He had caught Joan Wallin in extreme trajectory, so to speak. She also looked as good as ever. And then too, he was probably already getting a contact high.

"Well!" he said.

"You're supposed to play a little tonight. This is to experiment with—with a nice friend." She had an envelope on the glass-topped table, and now took a joint from it and handed it to him with a slight smile. "The thing is—not too many tokes. That's the secret. It's very powerful."

Long ago he had stopped smoking marijuana in order to contract his thought patterns to a size and shape that would be manageable, easily transportable, in the world at large. The alternative, after all, seemed to be some sort of retirement: smoking grass at home to have one's thoughts expand over the breadth of the entire planet—and beyond.

But he took two or three tokes and everything turned into some fabled dimension. Joan Wallin was real, with a figure and a face and a certain skin tone that held his blood. Yet there was a kind of lassitude, too. He ended up stretched out on the sofa, with his head in her lap. His thoughts took on the color of legend.

"You're like Aphrodite, or Ishtar."

"You just like my breasts."

"No, you've got an aura. You put a person into a frame of mind."

"You're stoned. Would you like to know something about my breasts, though?"

"We've been in bed together, remember? We've been on the floor together; we've been in the water together."

"That's not what I'm talking about. See, they're quite big. They're big enough for breast-fucking."

"What's that?"

"Well, see, I push them together and you fuck them until you're gonna come and if I feel like it I take you in my mouth."

"A woman should never talk like that."

"Why not?"

"Because it defiles her sacred mysteries." He was smiling again, though perfectly serious. "You have a beautiful body; you're possessed of a generous frame of mind. You should *never*, as a matter of *policy*, talk dirty."

"Okay, I just thought it might be fun."

He sat up now and went over to the windows to watch Columbus Avenue, lit up and going its nightly way. The city had a certain rigor of routine but it wasn't the soul at rest. Then again, that wasn't what life was about—rest. When he turned from the window and looked back at the sofa, Joan Wallin was gone.

In another moment, lingering at her bookcase, realizing how stoned he was now, he heard the Marvin Gaye album come on in the bedroom and knew she was in there, calmly, quietly ready for the happiness express. What he wanted was to lay his cheek on the satin inside of her thigh. It seemed like a good thing to do.

When he walked into the bedroom, he found that she already had a candle lit and lay naked on the bed on her side with one knee up.

"Hi," she said. "Do you want more grass?"

"No, thanks," he said, sitting down on the chair and looking at her.

Her body felt wonderful next to his body: each touch seemed to occur in multiple dimensions—in words and legend and memory as well as in the fleshly moment.

Their bodies were balm to one another, a kind of sacrament, and each instant now, of tongue or touch or the texture of hair, seemed to engrave itself in some eternity or other. Eternity, he knew, was what happened when the present became unfettered of the gravity of a single identity. It was in the transference from the one into the other.

"See, like this," she said.

It was sort of ridiculous, but not possible to resist, not now, when the clock had struck thirteen and the mouse had run away with the house.

17

"I feel like ice cream," she said. Her head was resting on his chest. "Let's go out and get some."

"Maybe we should get married." It was the marijuana speaking. A man who was stoned wished to spend his whole life secure in the contours of a sexual treat. The problem was the sexual climax, coming. It hurt to leave it too long. Sooner or later, it was over; and it was over now. Fucking wasn't a career. On the other hand, it was the only way to be in a perfect one-to-one relationship with the outside world.

"Where did you learn about that?" James asked.

"I saw it in a porno film on cable. Do you like it?"

"Sure. It was great."

"Let's get dressed."

He let his arm release her into the room. It was true: he couldn't seem to get enough of her. Perhaps this was the original dilemma behind cannibalism. Eat the girl and maybe it will go away. Yes, this was the space program, the space channel, that was broadcasting through him right this moment. Christ, how many more years did he have before his teeth fell out, his eyes got blurry, his hearing faltered, and women began looking at him as though he were a kitchen sideboard? Well, he had definitely slipped between the cracks this time. Joan Wallin was an anniversary of—ice cream, maybe?

She was dressing.

"Come on, sleepy head. It's Saturday night. We need ice cream."

"I'm up." He rousted himself into his pants and shirt, socks and shoes. He was devout, with come stains and disheveled hair, in a mood of perfect satiety, in the groove.

She had put on her overcoat, although the night had been mild. "Let's have a little taste before we go," she said.

Finished dressing, he ran his pocket comb through his hair a few times and sat down on the living-room sofa, undoing his cashmere scarf from his tweed jacket. His cells had been rinsed tonight; he felt light again, aerial. He traded the joint with her a few times; and then the front door opened and Allen Schweitzer came in.

Seeing the director suddenly like this alarmed him. He saw into his physical textures the tight grid of his fibers.

"Well, the lovebirds," Schweitzer said ambiguously, shedding a trenchcoat onto the back of the chair beside the door.

Joan Wallin stood up, as if in some alarm herself. "Oh, Allen. We're just going out."

"Can I have a hit? I'm already wired. Smooth, I hope."

Joan Wallin passed him the joint.

"Yeah, it's nice," James said as a sort of peace offering to the room.

"I didn't ask you," Schweitzer said, not looking at him.

His stomach went into a roil of panic. He had gotten stoned and had fun with his friend and now God had sent an ambassador of wrath. "That's all right. I volunteered the info to put you at your ease."

"Go fuck yourself, Redding," Schweitzer said, toking up beside the poster for his film *Revved.*

"Hey, what is this?" Joan Wallin said, standing between Schweitzer and James, who was sitting. Now James had to say something back.

"I'm sure I don't know," he essayed, figuring he might assuage Schweitzer with an impersonation out of drawing-room comedy.

"That's because you're an asshole," Schweitzer said, drawing deeply, still at the door.

Joan Wallin was looking between them now—into a middle distance like someone caught in an unpleasant magnetic field. James stood up.

"Back off, asshole," Schweitzer said without looking at him.

He *was* on *something,* that was clear. James decided to stay with his neutralizing persona for a moment longer. Eliminate all thoughts of violence—either from or to Schweitzer—and see if he could detoxify the room. He strolled over to the poster, keeping his own body movements studiously unaccented. "You know what I liked about *Revved?*" he said, passing Joan Wallin and laying a hand lightly on Schweitzer's navy blue crewneck sweater at the shoulder.

He had invited Schweitzer's more benevolent attention, planning to lie a little. Instead he went reeling down the side of the wall and a cluster of stars broke inside his sensorium—as vivid as a comic strip clout—and then another cluster. *Pow! Pow!* He saw stars, twice, and as it happened to him, considered it amazing. Then he had his back against the wall and Schweitzer at a remove of four or five feet, with Joan Wallin pushing the director away from him farther still until he smacked her open-handed across the face and she fell down in her overcoat. He looked over at James.

"Just really be a pussycat now and come over here for more."

This was Schweitzer's movie, all right, the moment when the auteur asserted his eminent domain, plotwise, billing-wise, etc. At the same time, the two smacks on the jaw had sent James sojourning into the recesses of his past. One afternoon in the Trinity locker room when he had seen stars for the first time: those clusters, like fireworks, across the slopes of the decades.

He felt the side of his face, took a deep breath for courage, and took a couple of casual, almost jaunty steps toward Schweitzer. Smiling, he said, "You see, Allen, the problem is..." and he shot his right foot into the general vicinity of Schweitzer's nuts. The director oofed, doubled over, and then looked up and James hit him with his right fist on the side of his face.

This made him sit down on the floor beside the glass-topped table.

"Yo, Rocky!" he said smiling to James. "Now get your ass outa here before I break your back."

"Right, Allen. As soon as you get up. What the fuck's wrong with you?"

"You wanna pay for this place, then you can come up and screw. Otherwise, back off motherfucker because I'm picking up the tab."

Schweitzer was out of breath. So was James.

"It's my choice, Allen," Joan Wallin said suddenly, having picked herself up from the floor. She had "come down" now and looked psychically, if not physically, bruised, although he might be seeing her in a different, adrenalized light. "Who do you think you are?"

"I'm the candy man, babe," Schweitzer said and started chuckling.

James sat down on the sofa beside Joan Wallin. He should have hit Schweitzer harder. He was confused. His mouth hurt. He was suddenly very, very tired.

"Get outa here!" Schweitzer shouted at him. He was still sitting on the floor with his feet in front of him. "I'm really gonna kick your ass."

"Listen, I'm not playing some *role* in your fucking fantasy life."

"Let's get out of here," Joan Wallin said, standing up beside him.

He looked up at her and then stood up too. She was right. It was time to go.

"Don't bring him back here again," Schweitzer shouted to her as she closed the front door.

In the elevator, she took a Kleenex out of her coat

pocket, wet it with her tongue, and wiped the side of his mouth, which now felt swollen. "You're a little bloodied."

"He's *crazy*."

"They turned down his movie today; I thought he'd gone to London."

"Why did he hit me like that?"

"Because he's jealous of you. He doesn't care about me anymore except as some sort of sister or mother or something. He doesn't look at anything over eighteen these days."

They went to Ruelles and sat down at a table and ordered drinks. He was still out of breath. He saw himself beating Schweitzer; he saw Schweitzer beating him.

After two drinks each, they left Ruelles and walked down Columbus and then west and on up Broadway. They stopped for espressos at Larry's by Shakespeare & Co. Now he tried to say to her what he had made the trip in from Connecticut to say.

"Look, I'd seen you in that bookstore a few times before; I'd sort of noticed this very beautiful woman sitting at a desk, sometimes typing, in the middle of this public place. Anyway..."

"Yes?"

His eyes darted back to hers. She was impatient with this, sapped by the night as much as he was. "The point is I've got good eyesight and I walk all over New York and you've got to be one of the ten best-looking women in the whole throng of eight million, maybe one of the top five. And that's got to be a heavy burden. It's mythological. Diana. Aphrodite. Helen of Troy. Whoever it is: the well-known gangster of love. And there's not a damn thing you can do about it. Men are going to be this heavy traffic factor. They're going to see something in you that you don't really see and they're going to disappoint you and you're going to..."

"Disappoint them?" She looked gravely over their table at him.

"You have to. Because you're human, even though the look you have will clear a man's mind and shine up his senses. That's why painters paint beautiful women. It refreshes the senses to see someone beautiful. It makes you feel young again. I'm forty years old and I've been behaving like I'm nineteen."

"I thought you were enjoying yourself quite a bit," she said, with a sudden edge of petulance, and looked up from where the waiter had just put down their second espressos. "But that's not something you want to admit."

"Oh, I'll admit it. I'll admit it." He looked from her through the plate-glass window at the nighttime Broadway passersby.

"Yeah, you'll admit it," she answered in a still harsher tone. "You're so typical, you know that? I mean, ever since junior high school, I've been going around with different versions of the same guy. And none of you, not *one,* knows anything about—not just women, I mean forget it, you don't have a clue...but about yourselves..."

Suddenly he saw again Mary Rosen's trip across their junior high school classroom to pick up her paper at the teacher's corner desk and the audible gasp as the male half of the class noticed how she had filled out. So here he was, maybe, sitting with such a woman a little farther down the line.

"...Not even yourselves. Not *one* of you..."

He could tell she felt self-conscious now in their public surroundings. He drank up his second espresso and put enough money to cover their bill on the table. Then they were walking on Broadway again, and she was clearly angry, the first time he'd seen her so. Their bubble had burst. She wasn't Ishtar, just a mortal young woman disappointed, sad maybe too, behind her anger. Too bad. Too bad about everything. She walked quickly, keeping her eyes aimed ahead.

"You've got two brains, all of you: the one in your head, and the one in your cock. And they don't get along. In fact, it's like they're complete strangers, they haven't been introduced at all, but they keep passing each other in the bathroom mirror. But they don't say hello, let alone anything else. I really pity you, you're so fucking pathetic!"

He caught the flash of her glance as they stepped up onto the corner of Eightieth Street. Her eyes looked red now and he had no idea what to do.

"I knew who you were and what you were all about. Allen knows you're married. You're not exactly anonymous at this point. So why was I so nice to you?—that's the real question; why I feel I have to be this fabulous fuck..."

"No, you didn't have to be..." His jaw ached. He had, in the end, so little knowledge of her life and larger identity.

"Wait a second." She had stopped under a darkened movie-theater marquee. "You see me and decide we should get together, right? And I'm flattered because I saw your movie and—whatever. Forget it." She looked at him grimly and started walking again.

But he owed her at least whatever it was she was getting at, wherever it was she wanted to go now. "You must really be tired of this kind of scene."

"Men aren't straight with themselves," she said. Now she turned east, toward her building. "They flatter themselves. They want Miss America, that girl Vanessa, you know, but with a degree in art history so they can go to the right parties. At bedtime, though, you can forget the degree."

They passed a glassed-in, elegantly appointed restaurant with only a few customers at one or two candlelit tables. It was long past midnight and the place had closed.

"I can see how you could not like me," he said. "But I—"

"And it really doesn't matter to you, does it?" she interrupted.

Was he really so far gone as that? He had done something entirely for himself, thrown away the rulebook he had played by up to then as if it were a quaint piece of superstition. Maybe he'd only played by it before, in any case, because he was afraid of jinxing his karma. Then he found money. He'd done everything he was supposed to do. He deserved a fling. A fling? He wouldn't be picking up a tab of any kind for this, or not from her. He had the ache in his jaw but that was from Schweitzer, who, whatever else you could say about him, was involved enough to hit him. The rules had gotten so blurred, as if the money was water over ink.

"I guess I don't know anything about you," he said hopelessly.

"That's okay," she answered. "Don't worry about it. My father has a hardware store and he loved me. I've always been much too nice to men." Now her tone shifted out of the momentary buoyancy. "Or maybe not. I don't even know. Maybe not."

At her building, he stood with her just east of the lighted entrance, both of them silent for a moment, as if trying to realize some elusive weight in the moment, some parting definition.

"You're a good person," he ventured finally, meaning it, as nearly as he could tell. "You've been really so—generous." Because she had been, in her way.

She was looking up toward Central Park. What more was there for him to say? "I hope you don't just specialize in affairs. You're worth more than that. You really are."

Her eyes flashed suddenly at him. "Thanks *a lot.* Just get outa here before I get really mad." She looked up the street again.

Fair enough. "Okay, Joan. Thank you." He had been about to kiss her on the side of her face when she moved out of range.

"Just get the fuck away from me, will you!" she yelled at him.

He realized he'd called her by her name for the first time and then his gut squeezed with a sudden fright. Simultaneously, for the second time that night, he felt the blunt disorientation of a physical blow, as if an interior television had suddenly disappeared—her fist glanced off the side of his face.

"Hey!" he yelled, astounded, covering his face and backing against the front of the building.

"Go fuck yourself!" she answered. "Fucking scumbag!" When he looked again, she had disappeared into her building.

James walked slowly downtown past the darkened Museum of Natural History where Paul loved to go to the carpeted minerals room with its glassed-in, lit-up exhibits. He felt half-numb, and yet, at the same time, his insides seemed to be racing, chafed with fright, and guilt, and humiliation. He listened to his own heels in the deserted night. It was too late now to pick up his car. He continued down Central Park West and then, on an impulse, turned down Seventy-sixth Street. Reva had a town house on the uptown side of the street between Central Park West and Columbus Avenue. He'd been there once and it would provide a point of reference, a familiar of some possible comfort in the abysmal upheaval of the night.

Going by the building, he saw that the lights were still on on the second floor, Reva's living room, and he could hear strains of Beethoven's *Emperor* Concerto coming from inside. It was close to three in the morning. He walked up the steps to the doorway and rang the buzzer.

"Yes?" the voice said on the intercom.

"Reva?"

"Yes?"

"It's James Redding."

"Oh, for God's sake." The buzzer rang and he was admitted into the inner chamber of the entrance. In another moment, Reva opened the inner door, dressed from head to toe in black motorcyclist leather, with her hair in some kind of studied punk disarray.

"I was in the neighborhood," James told her, involuntarily smiling, "and heard you were up. I had no idea you were into S & M."

"You really are freaking out," Reva answered seriously, standing in the doorway. "That's really tough. Okay, come in. Did somebody do something to your mouth or what?"

"Not too serious, I hope."

Reva's living room was on the second floor and he followed her up there and into the thick of the Beethoven. The leather pants fit her very tightly. In her living room, he sat down in a rattan chair while she went into the kitchenette in a corner of the room divided off by a bar.

"Have you met Blair, James? Blair, this is James Redding, one of my clients. Turn down the music, will you, sweets?" Reva was yelling.

James exchanged pantomimed hellos under the thunderous music with a slight, very pale man with a shock of very black hair that hung over his forehead and left eye. He was dressed in what appeared to be white pajamas. The music lowered, Blair went down the corridor and into a room at the floor's other end.

"Blair and I are writing a movie together," Reva

told him in her normal voice now. "Listen, what do you want to drink?"

"Nothing. I'm really sorry to bother you. Can I sleep on the couch and get outa here in the morning? My car's in a parking garage that doesn't open until six."

"Sure," she said, coming out from behind the bar and looking at him with a concern completely incongruous with her outfit. "You can sleep in the guest room downstairs. What's going *on* with you? Well, wait a minute. Shall we *not have* this conversation? You look just terrible. You want to go to sleep?"

"Reva, thanks."

"Listen, anything for a client." She turned and said, "Follow me." As he followed her down the stairs, she added, "*Almost* anything, okay?"

"No problem," he answered, confused.

She led him into a small bedroom off the first floor foyer. The single bed was neatly made up with a baby blue tasseled bed-cover. He was very tired, aching all over now, and the sight of this old-fashioned asylum was a relief.

"The bathroom's right here," Reva told him, pointing to a door inside the room. "That's the way we should do it, James. We shouldn't have this conversation, okay? I'm sure it's the right thing."

The deal with Reva. Strictly business, no real intimacy unless, he supposed, you decided you wanted to go kinky. Reva Makepeace will beat the shit out of you and not talk about it in the morning. But he'd already taken care of that option for tonight. "I believe you. This is very nice of you, Reva. I'll be out in the morning."

"Just don't wake me up. I'm gonna sleep in tomorrow. *Comprenez?*"

"Got it," he said, and she turned to go.

He left Reva's just after ten the next morning and walked over to Larry's. As far as he had been able to make out in Reva's bathroom mirror, the swelling in his jaw was only slightly visible now. The day was sunny and benevolent and, after two cups of coffee, he walked up the east side of the avenue. It was the solitude of New York he was hungry for: the spectacle that kept the front part of the mind occupied and allowed the rest of it a kind of respite.

However, somewhere in the Eighties he saw an old lady crossing the Broadway traffic island and greeting other old men and women, sunning themselves on the island benches. She was frail, yet sprightly, dressed in a blue woolen dress with a large leather handbag on one bony arm, but something in her greeting to one after another of her friends on the benches reminded him of Stephanie. Her smiling greeting seemed full of his younger daughter's affection for people. He had made such a mess of his life.

18

"So," Betty said that night in the darkness as they lay in bed, "how was it?"

"What?"

"Your trip into town, of course."

"Pretty bad, I guess."

"Do you still love her?"

"Still?"

"Well?"

"I'm a goddam middle-aged man and I'm—"

"Oh stop! What about me? You can go on and on; I have to do Jane Fonda and become an acrobat just to stay where I am."

"You look great."

"Thanks a lot. Coming from you, that means a lot."

"I started to say something..." He hadn't been sure, even a moment ago, what it was. "I guess..."

"Yes?"

There was a noise from the wall.

"What was that?" Betty said.

"I think Lisa turned in her bed... I'm an old man and nobody loves me."

"James, grow up."

"I love being counseled by another midlife nut..."

"Shut up!" She turned her back to him. Then, a moment or two later: "I can just see this girl. She had big boobs, right?"

He started to laugh, weakly.

"I knew it."

"Sometimes I think society really is falling apart."

"All this political crap. You know you're *not* Tom Hayden."

"Have you got Jane Fonda on the brain or what?"

"She's got to watch out or she's going to go the stringy route, like Nancy Reagan."

"Good point."

They were silent for a minute.

"If you ever fuck her again, I'm leaving."

"You don't have that to worry about, okay? But let me ask you something. How do I know you won't fuck Tony or somebody else again?"

"Women are different."

"Right. Women are different."

"They *are*."

He lay in the darkness for a moment, smiling for no reason. He touched her shoulder and then took his hand away again.

"Underneath it all, did you ever figure I'm just really tired of having all these bitches call the shots while I sit there minding my manners, my ego erased, sitting on my hands..."

"And having an affair with some bimbo who doesn't intimidate you. How reassuring for your ego!

I mean everybody has to make a living, don't they? I mean *don't they?* Isn't that just selfish?"

"And you're not?"

"No, I'm not! I married you and lived with you for twenty years with nothing and took care of you and your children and practically had a nervous breakdown trying to be a painter, too. I'm not selfish and if you think so just get out of here!"

She was sitting up in bed now and crying.

"You guys?" It was Lisa, outside their bedroom door.

"Lisa, I want you in your bed right now," he said.

"Are you all right?" she answered quietly.

"Yes, we're fine. We'll talk in the morning."

"You guys, can I come in?"

"Lisa, it's bedtime," he said as decisively and loudly as he could without waking up Stephanie and Paul.

"O-*kay*," she said.

Betty was still sitting up, her body silently, irregularly heaving with sobs.

He sat up and took her gently into his arms, remembering Joan Wallin's man with two brains. Yet with Betty, hadn't there been at least some traffic between the two? Maybe not a deep dialogue, but surely, over the past twenty years, the two had passed some notes, and maybe even cracked each other up once or twice: "Brain one to brain two... Come in, Charlie." For brain one and brain two, after all, would surely recognize in her someone out there in whom they could *both* place the burden of their trust.

"I love you," he told her. "I really do."

"No," she sobbed, "you don't."

"I do," he said, and held her. A tear fell from her

and onto his cheek. The tear fell down toward his mouth and he caught it with his tongue, warm and salty.

James woke as dawn was breaking on Monday morning. He had had a dream about Paul. His son had come to him exhausted somehow and needing James to get him to his bed.

"I think I'll take a rest, Dad," Paul had told him in a shallow voice in the dream. He couldn't think of a less characteristic line—Paul drove himself restlessly, relentlessly. But it touched James that his son would show this side of himself to him.

It was the kind of intimacy he had never quite managed with his father and now his father was gone. You didn't have forever, that was a piece of the news. But that didn't mean he didn't talk with him, argue with him viscerally most every day. And it didn't mean he couldn't still see his father's wry, condescending smile.

"Get to the point, Jamie. Get to the point."

It wasn't easy to explain to his father that he preferred a visceral, humanly rounded evasiveness to the razor-sharp strategies he had witnessed in his office and household. So, after all, he had his personal history: for better or worse, the pain and pleasure were etched into the grooves of his nervous system. And surely that counted for something. He had taken his father to heart, into gut, and the mistakes he had made were at least modified ones, he hoped, as opposed to simple repetitions.

Now Betty stirred beside him in bed and then

turned on her side away from him—her "pilgrim soul," his trusting, steadfast companion on the journey...Like two wanderers in a national desert of desiccated "success stories," their problem was how to keep contact with a water source. First they had wandered off with the rest of their generation. Yet the sixties, as long as they lasted, were like a single moment, transparent, luminous, and then suddenly, irrevocably, gone.

Then they had had children, finding at least part of the solution in a family. And subsequently he had worked his way back into the fold. The prodigal son returns—and lo, the welcoming committee is now made up almost exclusively of women. Then too, even after the asperities of their sixties lifestyle, he seemed to have retained the rich boy's usual problems with entitlement.

Just now, however, was like that moment in the writing of a play, somewhere beyond the halfway mark, when there is a sudden intimation of the whole design. Now this character who might have loomed preposterously large—he himself?—would be subsumed, perhaps even given a back seat, in the demands of the overall structure.

To do that with one's life! An aesthetician's sudden brainstorm. In writing, it was the moment when all the talent and craft and stamina one had developed would be tested. Now awake with urgency, James got up out of bed, put on his robe, and walked from their bedroom into the bathroom, switching on the light and studying his face in the mirror. He shut the door, locked it, and ended up sitting down in his robe on the toilet seat cover.

The choice of a form could be, after all, also the determination of one's nervous system. If, for instance, you could only go so far with laughter—well, then, you might choose not to tell another joke. In another moment, he got up again and walked back into their bedroom. It would be another half an hour before the kids would start waking up for school. He walked over to the window and looked into the dim early dawn, surprised to see the first translucent veil of frost over their lawn.